the tragic age

the

STEPHEN METCALFE

tragic

A NOVEL

age

St. Martin's Griffin ☙ New York

THE TRAGIC AGE. Copyright © 2015 by Stephen Metcalfe. All rights reserved. Printed in the United States of America. For information, address St. Martin's Press, 175 Fifth Avenue, New York, N.Y. 10010.

www.stmartins.com

Library of Congress Cataloging-in-Publication Data

Metcalfe, Stephen
    The tragic age / Stephen Metcalfe.—1st Ed.
        p. cm.
    ISBN 978-1-250-05441-8 (hardcover)
    ISBN 978-1-4668-5735-3 (e-book)
    1. Teenage boys—Fiction.   2. Friendship—Fiction.   I. Title.
    PS3563.E833T73 2015
    813'.54—dc23

                                2014034641

St. Martin's Griffin books may be purchased for educational, business, or promotional use. For information on bulk purchases, please contact the Macmillan Corporate and Premium Sales Department at 1-800-221-7945, extension 5442, or write to specialmarkets@macmillan.com.

First Edition: March 2015

10 9 8 7 6 5 4 3 2 1

Ours is essentially a tragic age, so we refuse to take it tragically. The cataclysm has happened, we are among the ruins.

—D. H. LAWRENCE

the
tragic
age

1

Pick a subject. Grab a word or headline or rumor. Read about it. Google it. Wiki it. Search and surf it. Stuff it. One site leads to another and then another. A new subject or word or phrase grabs your attention. It takes the place of the first one and you follow that trail, moving on and on, subject to subject, site to site, skimming the surface, never really digging deep, adhesive picking up lint, on and on until you've forgotten what it is that got you started in the first place.

In real time. In real life.

In Antarctica, an iceberg larger than the entire city of Chicago breaks off a glacier and begins floating happily across the southern ocean toward Argentina. Unimpressed, suicide bombers in Afghanistan, Iran, Syria, Pakistan, and Mozambique blow themselves up, killing both neighbors and complete strangers.

Again.

The market crashes. Reforms. Crashes.

And so on.

An Indian billionaire builds a twenty-seven-story house

overlooking the slums of Mumbai and then abandons it because it has bad karma. A neuroscientist shoots seventy people in a Memphis auditorium. Another neuroscientist tells us you can't blame him, it's just the way his brain is wired.

There are Asian carp in the Great Lakes and walking snakes in Florida. In Australia they're losing the Great Barrier Reef to horned starfish while in France bus drivers abandon their vehicles and go on strike, shutting down public roadways, because their uniform pants are too tight.

In Switzerland, they're crashing subatomic particles into each other at the speed of light, searching for the glue of life. Why not? It's better than predicting global disaster, designing new varieties of pink slime, and replicating human proteins in cloned goats.

Breathe in, breathe out.

Enough of real life. Take a break. Turn on the television. Television is pretend life. And with basic cable you can watch it all day long. *Desperate Housewives. American Idol.* An idol is a cult image, venerating the spirit it represents. The cult that is American venerates desperate singing morons. Shooting cops. Forensic cops. Female cops. Wisecracking cops. Singing cops. Cops wearing sunglasses. Emergency room doctors. Student doctors. Drug-addicted doctors. Plastic surgeons on Viagra and steroids. Meth dealers. Zombies. Vampires.

Reality shows. What is reality? Is it tanned Italians in a Jersey beach house? Barbie dolls married to has-been rock stars? Housewives of Miami, New Jersey, Beverly

Hills, Greater Pomona, and Baton Rouge? Or is it Las Vegas pool parties, celebrities in rehab, and politicians on *Meet the Press?*

We are all avid spectators at a car crash.

I should know. My name is Billy Kinsey. I'm seventeen years old. I watch a lot of TV. Often all night long.

I live in a nice house. It has five bedrooms, eight bathrooms, and a four-car garage. More than enough room for three people. We have a nice view. When I come out to stand in our backyard in the morning, I can see the Pacific Ocean in the distance. The Coronado Islands are somewhere to the south. Hawaii is two thousand miles to the west. Hollywood is . . . we won't mention that again.

Ours is the kind of neighborhood where men and women in expensive workout clothes walk expensive designer dogs that don't shed. People know the dogs' names but they don't know each other's. The dogs take dumps on random lawns and sniff each other's assholes. This is a dog's way of introducing himself to his friends. It's how they tell each other how they're feeling, what they've eaten lately, and whether they're dangerous, pregnant, or just plain crazy. The nose does not lie, and when you get right down to it, maybe we should all be sniffing each other's butts as well.

This is also the kind of neighborhood where on weekends a lot of people who should know better put on uncomfortable helmets, skintight Lycra emblazoned with European logos, and go riding around on titanium bicycles that cost as much as small cars. Sometimes they come to a stop and can't release their shoes from the pedals and fall over. They lie there groaning, still attached to their bikes.

For those who don't bike, there's a pleasant little Ferrari dealership in the village. There's also a Maserati dealership, a Rolls-Bentley dealership, a Ferrari dealership, and a Lamborghini dealership. There's a Tesla dealership. A Tesla is an energy-saving, ecofriendly, fully electric sports automobile. In this case, one that has a carbon-fiber body, goes from zero to sixty in 3.7 seconds, and costs over a hundred and ten thousand dollars. Talk about friendly.

We used to have a Segway dealership selling two-wheeled, self-balancing, personal transports but then the British billionaire owner of the company inadvertently drove his off a cliff and died. Sales inexplicably declined.

It wasn't always palm trees, luxury cars, and the blue Pacific. Till the age of four, I lived in Tulare, California, in the San Joaquin Valley. The crop of choice is hay. People enjoy beer, methamphetamine, and looking for bodies in irrigation canals. Tourists come for the retail outlets.

I've seen photos in old family photo albums. Our house was small. Dad—*Gordon*—worked construction. Mom—*Linda*—was a housewife. There's one photo that shows me as a toddler playing in a pile of bagged mulch. In the foreground, Mom is planting nonindigenous flowers that will inevitably die. She looks happy doing it. Her hair is brown and messy. She's on her knees and you can tell she's having fun getting her hands dirty.

On March 18, 1999, Dad won 37 million dollars in the California lottery and everything changed.

Fate.

Seven months later, a stranger in a bowling alley told Dad that if he was smart, he'd invest in a company called Qualcomm. This was the equivalent of a guy in a bowling shirt giving Jack the magic beans to the golden goose for free. Qualcomm is now the biggest producer of semiconductors and cell phone technology in the world.

Inevitable events.

A year after that, worn out by friends with business ideas, acquaintances asking for loans, and complete strangers showing up on the doorstep begging for handouts, Mom and Dad moved south to the fourteenth-wealthiest community in the United States, a place where begging is discouraged, loans are kept private, and where, even though they shared similar physical characteristics with the residents, they were as different as Tagalog-speaking hermaphrodites from Mars.

Providence. Zahmahkibo from the Book of Vonnegut and Bokonon.

We've acclimated.

Mom's name is still Linda but Linda is now a lean, tawny blonde with a tan and perfect nails. Mom is now part of this group of women who call each other all day long, making and breaking appointments and talking behind each other's backs.

"Well, I think it's silly," Mom will say. "She's spending

more on the invitations than she is on the— It's supposed to be for charity, right?"

Stuff like that. They also play tennis, meet for lunch, do yoga, and shop.

"Hold on, Jen."

Mom always interrupts her phone call when she sees me, like she wants me to know that I'm every bit as important as whoever it is she's talking to.

"Hey, honey," she'll say. "Sleep well?"

"Great," I'll say. "Like a baby."

"I thought I heard you up."

"Not me."

"Where are you going?"

"Siberia by bus."

"Take your cell phone!"

And then she's back into her conversation, not even realizing that I wouldn't own a cell phone if you paid me. Fact.

Cell phones emit radiofrequency energy, a form of nonionizing electromagnetic radiation. Why take the risk?

Sidebar.

When you answer the phone there's usually someone on the other end who wants to talk. Why take the risk?

She tries, Mom. She really does. It's her nature to. But for Dad—*Gordon*—it's officially too late. It'll be a Sunday afternoon and we'll be in the garage next to the Range Rover, the Jaguar XJ Supersport, and the customized Ford F-150 pickup that Dad likes to drive because it reminds him of his "roots." Dad will have recently gotten back from riding his titanium bike, and after complaining about all the cars that don't stop for downed riders, he'll have been going on about his impoverished youth for at least ten minutes now, all because, on some nostalgic whim, he's bought a push lawn mower.

"Give me one good reason," he'll say, "why I should pay some Mexican twelve bucks an hour to mow the lawn when I have a kid who does nothing but sit around on his ass all day doing nothing!"

Actually I don't just sit around on my ass all day doing nothing. I sit around on my ass and read. I like knowing things. Just don't make me talk about them.

Dad doesn't read or know anything and all he does is talk.

"When I was your age, I worked, kiddo. I didn't have the advantages you have!"

On and on he'll go. At some point along the line, Dad—*Gordon*—decided he'd *earned* everything we have, and after a successful career in the construction biz followed by a brilliant investment career, he decided it was time to smell the roses, watch the kids grow, and coach a little baseball.

Point of reference.

Baseball must be the most beef-witted game ever invented.

I'm, like, eight, and Dad has made me join Little League. And they have me in this stupid uniform which comes complete with what Aldous Huxley in his dystopian novel *Brave New World* referred to as a "prole hat." Prole, short for "proletariat." Meaning moron. Anyway, because I'm such a reluctant ball player, they've stuck me in right field and I'm standing there with this big, stiff, brand-new, expensive glove that Dad has bought me and all I can think about is when I'll finally get to go home. And then, wouldn't you know it, some dumb, fat kid actually hits the ball and it bounces through the infield and comes right toward me. And I'm not remotely paying any kind of attention, and even if I were I wouldn't be interested, and so it goes right past me. And all my so-called team-mates are screaming and their parents are screaming and Dad, who, yes, is "coaching a little baseball" and who looks even more ridiculous in his baseball uniform than I do, is screaming too.

"Billy, what's the matter with you! Goddammit, Billy! Get the goddamn ball!"

The only sane thing to do is ignore them all and so that's what I do. I just stand there, watching the dumb, fat kid run around the bases.

And now I'm seventeen and in the garage and nothing's really changed. Dad's still yelling.

"Good Christ Almighty, Billy, are you listening to me? Are you paying attention? Have you heard one goddamn word I've said?"

"Thirty," I'll say.

"What?"

"To mow the lawn. I want thirty dollars an hour. With a three-hour minimum."

This is called capitalism.

Dad will snort and make a face that says "You're so such an idiot, you're almost funny." He makes this face with Mom—*Linda*, his wife, my mother—a lot.

This is called derision.

"Anything else, your majesty?"

I stare at the lawn mower. The *hand* lawn mower that he—*Gordon*—wouldn't cut his toenails with.

A couple of hours later, I'll be in our backyard, which is lush and green and beautiful, and I'll be riding around on a brand-new tractor mower, the one we've traded the hand mower in for. Dad's the kind of guy who will upgrade anything mechanical at a moment's notice and call it a good investment. And maybe it's because the thought of this annoys me or maybe it's because it really *wouldn't* be a bad thing for me to push a mower, but I'll begin driving in this random, haphazard path across the lawn, leaving crazed swathes of uncut grass behind me.

"Billy, what the hell's the matter with you! Goddammit! Billy!"

I hate money. People who make nothing but money, make nothing.

Still.

It's money that pays for the drum room.

2

The drum room.

The drum room is on the lower level of the house. You might call this level the basement if a basement had inlaid wood floors, lath and plaster walls, and crown moldings. Dad had the drum room professionally soundproofed because not only was the noise driving him crazy, he was convinced it was stirring up the sediment in the cases of vintage Bordeaux that he had impulsively bought to put into the walk-in, climate-controlled wine cellar that came with the house.

My set is a Pearl Masterworks series. Black pearl. Double bass drums, a twelve-inch Tama Warlord Titan snare, four rack toms, and two floor toms, all tuned at two intervals apart. The set has six Zildjian cymbals; two rock rides, two custom crash, and a high hat.

My sound system is a Lyngdorf TDAI2200 Integrated Amp and Onkyo CS5VL SACD/CD player that plugs into a Pioneer S4EX speaker system.

Drum karaoke.

The very first concert was probably people beating logs

by the fire. The rhythms were the patterns that made up their natural world—wind, rain, stampeding hooves—and through these patterns, they experienced ecstasy.

What are my patterns?

Speed metal. Thrash. Ska punk. Progressive rock. Anything or anybody that makes me work. Neil Peart. Mike Portnoy. Shannon Leto of Thirty Seconds to Mars. Danny Carey of Tool. Stewart Copeland of The Police for simple precision. But my favorite drummer of all time is Avenged Sevenfold's Jimmy Sullivan aka the Reverend Tholomew Plague aka the Rev. Dead of acute drug and alcohol intoxication at the age of twenty-eight.

Better to drum yourself to death.

The soundproof room is small and insular and hot and it doesn't take long before I'll be dripping with sweat. A lot of times I strip down to my underwear or take my clothes off completely. My hands and bare feet blister and bleed and the blood and the sweat spot the drum heads. Drumming is the closest thing I know to mindlessness.

I would never ever play for people.

3

"Billy! Billy, hi!"

This is the Sunday morning that as I sit on the beach wall reading *Walden* by Henry David Thoreau, who I'm finding to be a pretentious, pedantic, sanctimonious, holier-than-thou, sheep-brained stiff, the tall, slim girl with the long, light red hair and the green eyes calls out to me. She's up on the road above the seawall. She's in running shorts and sports bra and has obviously been jogging and now she's stopped. She waves, hopping in place, the way runners do while waiting to pass out or for a traffic light to change.

My hand has gone up to cover the right side of my face, the way it always does when I'm startled or surprised. A port-wine hemangioma is a reddish to purple birthmark caused by dilated capillaries in the skin. Mine starts just to the right of my eye and spreads like a stain down and across most of my cheek.

The girl with the long, light red hair and the green eyes points at herself.

"Gretchen! Gretchen Quinn! We're back!"

Fact.

Shock is a response in the body's sympathetic nervous system. The heart jumps. Breath catches. Blood vessels in the brain contract, throwing off sparks.

The red-haired girl smiles again. She waves at me again. "See you at school!" And then she's off again, running. She has a beautiful, long stride.

I lower my hand. The side of my face pulses and feels hot. I feel as if *I'd* like a pond to run away to.

I hate it when people expect things of you. I just hate it.

4

"All hope abandon, ye who enter in!"

Dante Alighieri wrote *The Divine Comedy* in 1308. The most famous part describes the poet's journey through the nine circles of hell. He got it wrong.

Hell is high school.

High School High is a public school. Originally Mom and Dad wanted me to go to this big-deal private high school that cost about forty grand a year and where the students wear uniforms but I refused. I'd already gone to a big-deal private middle school that cost about fifty grand a year and I'd absolutely hated it. Being surrounded by oblivious, hormone-crazed nitwits is bad enough. Being surrounded by oblivious, hormone-crazed nitwits in identical blazers, chinos, and plaid skirts had made me want to climb an electrical tower and cauterize myself.

Still, we have a lot of well-to-do, self-entitled kids at good ol' High School High, and the ones that aren't, the ones that are mostly bused in and ignored, the social mutants, the Mexicans, and the black kids who have been recruited to play football and basketball, wish they were.

Because I wouldn't get a driver's license if they were giving them away, I ride a skateboard to school. I consider it nothing more than an acceptable means of transportation. If you ever see me hanging around a parking lot doing *ollies*, for God's sake, or attempting to destroy my testicles by sliding down a banister with the board *sideways*, please shoot me.

I will confess to the occasional game of chicken.

It's like this. At the top of a decent hill you wait until a car is coming up from the bottom. You take a moment to consider the fact that the wheel is a circular device capable of rotating on its axis. It's one of man's oldest and most important inventions. You push off, aiming down the middle of the approaching car's lane. You do a little side-to-side to establish a rhythm. The car is getting closer now and usually the driver is leaning on the horn. You go into a crouch to gain speed. The car swerves. You swerve with it. It starts to turn. Too late. You go into the grille. You hurtle forward into the windshield, which crumples with the force of your body. You're aware of the driver screaming as you're thrown up and over the roof and then you're airborne, aware of the street flying beneath you, aware of how rough it is and how much it's going to hurt your already badly broken bones when you land.

Of course, that isn't remotely what happens.

The car either stops, in which case you ride around it, or the car swerves and you keep going. Either way, you've won. Stupid, really. Crazy even. But here's the thing. Starting around the age of fourteen, human beings become certifiably insane. Really, they've done tests. A teenager's brain waves are the same as that of a psychotic's. They used to think this was a temporary condition, that if you made it to your twenties, you'd straighten out. But starting around the beginning of the twenty-first century, mostly due to the deleterious effects of twenty-four-hour global news coverage, not to mention the iPod, Netflix, and the Twilight Saga, young people started hitting puberty and never got over it. Ten percent of all teenagers today have been prescribed medication for depression. Eight out of every one hundred thousand teenagers commit suicide. Sixteen percent of all teenagers actively consider it. We are, as a generation, a bunch of deranged, isolated neurotics destined to live long lives of self-medicated, Internet-addicted lunacy. I'm not immune to the statistics but I do consider it a personal challenge to fight my generation's psychosis as much as possible.

And so I do.

I start by being not popular. The need for attention and celebrity based on questionable achievement is a dangerous drug. No. Better to avoid attention. Make no waves. Stay under the radar. Don't speak unless spoken to and then with as few words as possible. Do not volunteer. Do not join in. Get Bs and Cs, not As. Never raise your hand, and if called on, answer all questions with a puzzled expression. Run from the light. Keep to the shadows. Stay as far away as you can from the line of fire.

It doesn't always work.

"You haven't applied to college."

It's the second week back from summer vacation and I've been called into the guidance office. The guidance counselor, Miss Barber, is new this year. She's young and sort of attractive and she obviously thinks she can make a difference.

She'll get over it.

Right now, though, she has my transcript up on the computer screen in front of her and she has me on the spot.

"Well?" she says. "Why is that?"

"I thought I'd take some time off," I say.

"It seems to me you have been," she says. "Reading and math at a college level by the fourth grade. Over the top on your S10 series in fifth grade. You hit sixth, you disappear completely." She seems not so much puzzled as suspicious. "Care to explain?"

"It got tougher," I say.

"Mmm," she says. Which is a way of saying both something and nothing at the same time.

She studies the computer screen for a moment and then glances at me, eyes never quite settling on my face, not wanting to *stare*. One of the polite ones.

To consider.

We unconsciously distance ourselves from disfigurement, even when we know the condition is not contagious.

"Any ideas what you'd like to do, any plans for the future?" says Miss Barber.

"I'd like to find a deep cave and hole up in it for about eighty years," I say.

Actually, I don't say that.

"I'm not sure yet," I say. "But I'm working on it."

What I'd *like* to say is that planning for the future, any future, but especially one where it's predicted that by 2050 the worldwide population will level out and start dropping as if off a precipice, is ridiculous. This is because by 2030, thanks to out-of-control birth rates, bankrupt economies, and a global lack of natural resources, fresh water, and food, people will have begun getting very busy killing one another.

Just another thing to look forward to.

Miss Barber "mmms" again. She sits back in her chair. She taps a pencil. She looks at me as if *I'm* a question she's supposed to answer. "So how are things at home," she says. As if it's a *casual* question and not a fully charged death ray.

"Good," I say. "Really great."

"Get along with your parents?" she says.

"Mmm-hmm," I say. Which is a variation on "mmm."

"You're the only teenager I know that does," she says. Miss Barber looks down a moment and then she looks back up at me and I know exactly what's coming.

"May I ask about your sister?"

Dorie.

I'm eleven years old and I'm in a hospital room and my twin sister, Dorie, lies in a hospital bed. Even with her hair lost to chemo, she's really beautiful. She's pale, almost translucent, unblemished. Like a Dresden doll.

Point of reference.

A Dresden doll is tiny, collectible figurine whose body

is made of fabric, whose head is made of unglazed porcelain, and whose eyes are made of clear glass. Dresden is a city in Germany that was firebombed by Allied Forces at the end of World War II. A minimum of one hundred thousand people died. Most of them were civilians. Most of the civilians were women and children.

Sidebar.

Porcelain is inflammable. People aren't.

Dorie opens her eyes. It's silly how bright they are. Fever makes them this way. She sees me and smiles her Dorie smile.

"Hi, Billy," she whispers.

Acute lymphocytic leukemia is the most common type of leukemia in children.

"Mom and Dad say you're going to help me," Dorie says.

A bone marrow transplant replaces diseased blood cells with healthy cells from a compatible donor. Fraternal or *dizygotic* twins are often but not always compatible. Apparently I'm a very good match.

"You don't have to if it hurts," she says.

"I want to," I say. "I want you to get better."

"Me too," Dorie says. She holds out her hand to me and I take it. I hold her fingers tight in my palm.

Mom says Dorie and I came out of the womb together holding hands. Dorie came first, pulling me firmly but gently after her. I believe it. Dorie was always the brave one.

"Billy?"

I look up. Miss Barber is staring at me. I don't know

how long she's been waiting for me to speak. The side of my face feels cold and numb and my voice sounds far away, even to me.

"Yes?"

"We were talking about your sister?"

"Yes."

Miss Barber glances uncertainly at her notes. "I understand she was ill?"

"Yes."

"She's better now?"

As if people always get better.

"She's dead now."

Only sometimes they don't.

"I am *so* sorry."

People usually are.

"No problem."

I was only supposed to save her.

5

One of the unusual things about Mom—*Linda*—is that she always insists we have dinner together as a family several nights a week.

The housekeeper will cook something before she leaves and Mom will set the table and light the candles in the big dining room and she'll serve what the housekeeper has made, like pork chops in a chili-verde sauce, which is actually *really* good, as if she made it herself. Dad—*Gordon*—will sit at the head of the table, a bottle of insanely expensive cabernet in front of him, swirling his wineglass, as if he actually knows what he's doing. Mom and I will be on either side of him. Sometimes we'll all even try to get a little pleasant conversation going. It can be pretty nice, really. At least it's a nice idea.

But this is one of those nights when Mom clears her throat and smiles at us and you just know the evening is turning horrible.

"Well," Mom says. "Did anyone have an interesting day today?"

Dad and I share a quick look. I don't think Dad ever

has interesting days, and if he does, they're not the kind of interesting he's going to share with Mom. And so, just to be safe now, he doesn't say a word. Following in his footsteps, neither do I.

"All right," Mom says. "How about this? What's the best and worst thing that happened to each of us today?" Mom is trying to look cheerful. This is obviously some line of questioning she's gotten from a friend who probably got it from some daytime talk show where women discuss their feelings.

Dad, who *hates* discussing feelings, especially Mom's, sticks his nose into his wineglass and sniffs. This is called "catching the bouquet." It's a good way to stall for time if nothing else.

"All right," Mom says, still all pleasant. "I'll start. Betsy Mirrens broke her foot and will be off the tennis court for six weeks."

Dad frowns. "Betsy who?" You get the feeling that whoever she is, he doesn't like her.

"The Mirrenses." Mom sounds impatient. "We've joined them for any number of dinner parties."

Dad shrugs. "All we *do* is join people for fucking dinner parties." He takes a sip of wine and begins to gurgle it in the back of his throat. This is called "aerating." To aerate means to add oxygen. Oxygen changes things.

Mom, who doesn't like it when Dad starts tossing around F-bombs, is beginning to look sort of pinched and frustrated. I figure it's time to help her out.

"What's the best thing?" I say.

Success. Mom looks pleased.

"Thank you for asking. The best thing is ..." She pauses dramatically. "I got a clean bill of health from Dr. Knight today."

This makes Dad and me *really* share a look.

It's like this.

About two and half years ago Mom was getting a basic medical checkup and they found a lump in her left breast. Coming after Dorie, this news was a total bitch. They did a biopsy and it was cancer and so they did a lumpectomy and also took out her lymph nodes. Mom was in the middle of doing hormone therapy when they found another lump. This time they did a mastectomy, which removed all of her breast, and even though they did reconstructive surgery at the same time, she was pretty bummed out about it. This time she followed it up with chemo as well as hormone therapy. She lost most of her hair. She spent a lot of time vomiting.

Like Dorie.

For the last eight to ten months or so Mom's been looking and feeling pretty much like her old self which has been nice because it's made it easy for Dad and me to forget what she's gone through.

"Is he positive?" asks Gordon. Like he doesn't quite believe it.

"As positive as anyone can be about these things," says Mom. She eats a bite of pork chop. She chews it carefully. She swallows. She wipes her mouth with her napkin.

"So," she says. "Anyone else? Best thing, worst thing?"

Dad sighs. "I don't want to play this stupid game." He pushes his plate aside and tops off his wineglass.

Mom looks like he's slapped her. "All *right*," she says, her voice all tight and strained now. She turns to me. "Billy?"

I decide to lie. Really, it's such an easy thing to do.

"I didn't have anything bad happen," I say, because I am *not* going to tell them about Miss Barber. "But the best thing is sitting right here, having dinner with you guys."

Mom beams. She looks pleased. Really pleased. So does Dad. He actually smiles. "If that's the case, kiddo," he says, "you really need some new friends."

Success.

Everybody grins and chuckles as if that's the *last thing* in the world I need. Because who needs more friends when *obviously* I already have so many I've lost count? Who needs friends when we all have each other?

"Actually I *did* have something kind of funny happen today," says Dad.

It's not funny at all but the three of us have a good moment or two pretending it is. And then we sit there, pretty much in silence, aerating and changing, for the rest of the meal. For better or for worse, who's to say.

6

For some reason, usually after dinner, though sometimes later, Mom always asks me if I'm going to bed anytime soon.

"Sure am," I say. Even though I'm not.

"Sleep well," Mom says.

"Sure will," I say. Even though I won't.

The reality is I don't sleep much and Mom knows it. Several hours a night here and there. Sometimes not at all. I try but I just don't. I haven't since Dorie died. It's a problem.

Fact.

Insomnia is defined as the difficulty in getting to, and staying, asleep. Learned insomnia is when you worry about not being able to sleep, primary insomnia is when there's no reason for you not to sleep, and chronic insomnia is any insomnia that lasts for over a month. Sleep dread is when you're afraid to go to sleep to begin with. I have the entire package. So do the vast majority of institutionalized psychiatric patients.

Just another thing to look forward to.

Tonight, once Mom and Dad have gone to bed, I go back downstairs to the family room where the family never gathers, and with Dorie sitting on my shoulder, I watch TV far, far into the night, never sticking with any one thing for too long. I keep the sound low. Sometimes I turn it off altogether. I go back upstairs around four. I lie in bed. Maybe I doze a little. When Mom asks how I've slept in the morning I'll tell her what I always tell her.

Like a baby.

7

"Hammurabi!"

It's a Thursday, sixth period World History, the horse latitudes, and the teacher, Mr. Monaghan, knows he's going down with the ship.

"Hammurabi reigned over the Babylonian Empire until his death in 1750 B.C. And he did what, people? Anyone?"

No one is remotely paying attention. Mr. Monaghan, small, slight, possibly gay, and one of the few male teachers at High School High who wears a tie every day, and raises his voice like a tourist who thinks shouting will make him understood in a foreign language.

"He created *laws*, people! The code of Hammurabi. The fundamentals of which—"

As Mr. Monaghan turns and paces and lectures to the ceiling, I glance around. I see twenty-eight teenagers who look like they're taking a collective dump of tedium. It's as if their jeans, skirts, and underwear are down around their ankles and they're sitting on toilets with painful, constipated looks on their faces. Of course, part of this might be that no one, except me, has read the assignment. And I'm not about to admit to it.

"... two hundred eighty-two laws, written on twelve clay tablets in—what? Anyone?"

If Mr. Monaghan is waiting for an answer he's going to be waiting a very long time.

"Akkadian, people! The language of Babylon! The foundation of modern civilization!"

He might as well be *speaking* in Akkadian. If one moron brings an accusation against another moron, and that moron leaps into a river, if he sinks, the first moron shall take possession of his house. Some foundation of civilization. Maybe people have always been insane.

And now, just in time to prevent us all from killing ourselves, there's a knock on the door. Mr. Monaghan sighs. He looks discouraged. It must drive teachers crazy to have to spend so much time teaching something that no one really cares about. Of course, the study of ancient Babylon doesn't present a lot of job options to do anything else.

Mr. Monaghan crosses the front of the room, opens the door and steps out into the hallway. Everyone gives a collective sigh of relief. Maybe he won't come back. But then Mr. Esposito, the school principal, sticks his head in, wrinkles his brow, tightens his lips, and squints at us. It's like he's a displeased police detective and he's trying to decide whether or not we're worth making his day. Apparently we're not because after a second he ducks back out. You can hear him and Mr. Monaghan murmuring at one another. I can just see some papers change hands.

"Yes, all right, come in," Mr. Monaghan says. He steps back into the room. With the guy.

You feel a stir of interest in the room.

The guy is tall. He wears black jeans and a RAGE AGAINST THE MACHINE T-shirt with the sleeves cut off. He wears heavy motorcycle boots. The jeans, shirt, and boots look like a uniform on him. His dark hair is sort of long and wavy, a lot of it different lengths. He has steel closure rings in his left ear and one in his right eyebrow.

Hammurabi probably did too.

He has a barbed-wire tattoo spiraling down his ropy muscled right forearm.

Barbed wire signifies confinement.

He has brightly colored flower tattoos covering his left.

Flowers are symbols of youth, life, and victory over death.

He has woven strands of wire and leather worn loose around his neck. A metal scorpion dangles from it.

An amulet protects the wearer from harm.

"People," says Mr. Monaghan, "we have a new student joining us. This is"—and he reads from the paper—"Willard Twomey." Some of the morons in the class snicker at the name. The guy doesn't seem to notice.

"Take a seat, Mr. Twomey," says Mr. Monaghan. "We'll get you up to speed later."

Willard Twomey moves down the aisle and past me. He makes no eye contact with anyone. As if guided by radar, he steps over an outstretched foot. Some of the morons in the class snicker again. Willard Twomey's expression doesn't change.

None of this is happening, and if it is, he couldn't care less.

8

At the end of every day in front of good ol' High School High, there's always a line of vehicles clogging the street, waiting to pick up the younger kids who don't have rides or are too lazy to walk. Most of these vehicles are pricey SUVs, and behind the wheel of each of them there's usually a distracted, impatient soccer mom while in the backseat are crying babies, barking dogs, pissed-off toddlers, and sullen middle schoolers.

Fact.

There are over fifty thousand automobile fatalities in the United States every year.

Fact.

Two hundred thousand died at Hiroshima.

Conclusion.

A frazzled soccer mom in a five-thousand-pound sport utility vehicle is more dangerous than an atomic bomb. Really, they can get you anywhere, even in front of your own house. They can even be those who are closest to you.

Example.

I'm on my skateboard, at the end of the driveway, just coming home from school, when Mom almost takes me out with the Range Rover. The window is half open and she's on her cell phone, fumbling with her Bluetooth. "Hold on, Jane. No, nothing's wrong, I almost killed Billy."

She rolls the window down all the way.

"Billy, the Taylors are out of town. Would you get their newspaper and mail and put it in the house?"

"If they're gone, why are they getting a newspaper?"

"Because they don't want burglars to know that nobody's home."

"The paper was delivered this morning. It's been sitting there all day. Won't that tell burglars nobody's home?"

"Sweetie, I'm late for my Pilates, will you just do it?"

Mom holds out house keys and I take them.

"Wait—here's the security code."

She hands me a slip of paper.

"Thanks, hon. Oh, and feed the dog!"

And then she's off, driving away like a maniac, on the phone again. Mom I would *not* want to play chicken with.

The Taylors live up and across from us. Their home is a series of one- and two-story bunkers that look like an architect came in and said, Why don't we build a house that will take up the entire lot and have nothing in common with anything else on the street.

The Taylors' mail consists of a gas and electric bill, a couple of glossy catalogues, *Fortune* magazine, and some third-class trash. Their paper is the *L.A. Times*, which, like most newspapers, will soon be out of business.

The Taylors' security code is 7606 which—the height of brilliance—is their address on the street. When I punch in the code a metallic voice pipes up.

Security *on*.

The Taylors have gone off and left their miniature Getty Museum open to the public.

I punch in the code again to turn off the alarm. I put the mail and paper down on the foyer table with the other mail and papers. It's quiet. All you can hear is the barest whisper of the central air-conditioning. I look around. The Taylors' house is all corners and hard surfaces and weird furniture and it's about as hospitable as an airplane hangar. Just by looking at it you can tell everything cost a mint.

Something goes *yarp* and I jump. It's the Taylors' dog, I'd forgotten about it. It's a dachshund.

Point of reference.

Dachshunds were originally trained to hunt and kill badgers, which means that once upon a time they were ferocious little bastards.

However.

This one is so happy to have a visitor, it flops over on its back and, tail wagging furiously, urinates on itself. It's people who've done this to him. People do stuff like this to everything.

After I feed the Taylors' dog some canned goop from a cupboard in the kitchen, I decide to do a little more exploring. On the freestanding, granite-topped pedestal desk in the downstairs office I discover an unpaid American Express bill and an open box of Depends shields that offer to guard my manhood with man-style protection. Mr. Taylor is not only in credit card debt up to his eyeballs, he wears male diapers.

Who knew?

In the downstairs bathroom I check out the medicine cabinet. Mrs. Taylor takes antidepressants.

Who doesn't?

In the hallway there's a framed photo on the wall of Mr. Taylor holding a large, dead fish and another of Mrs. Taylor in a skimpy bikini. Both the fish and Mrs. Taylor's breasts look fake.

Whose aren't?

And then in the master bedroom I open the top drawer of a bureau and I find a diary. It's Mrs. Taylor's diary and I sit down and I begin to read.

Mrs. Taylor is having an affair. She's keeping the diary hoping Mr. Taylor will find it and ask about it. Only Mr. Taylor never asks about anything. Mrs. Taylor prays to God for help.

Good luck.

I close the diary, get up and go to the bureau to put it back. I have it exactly where it was in the drawer when my hand nudges something. I push aside the underwear that's covering it. I look at it. I take it very carefully in my hand and I lift it out. It's heavier and clumsier than I expect.

The etched letters on one side tell you it's a Glock .357 automatic. The letters on the other side tell you it gives you "the confidence to live your life."

It's the most beautiful thing in the house.

9

It's between morning classes when Deliza Baraza comes up to her locker, which for two, going on three years at good ol' High School High has been next to mine. I can actually feel her approaching. It's like there's a seismic pheromone shift in the hallway. Anything male begins to flutter and jerk. Deliza's father's a Mexican-American financier. Her mother's a former Telenuevo star. You wonder how they ever let Deliza out of the house. This morning she's done up in a sheer white blouse with a Peter Pan collar, a tiny cardigan sweater vest, a little tie, and a pleated short skirt. Her smooth dancer's legs are stuffed into white anklet socks and six-inch spike heels. Her dark hair is in pigtails and her makeup, which is always professionally perfect, is that of a toffee-colored geisha.

"Hey, Billy," she says. She has a deep, confident voice. Deliza only dates older guys. Rumor has it she charges them for the fun of it.

"Hey, D." I try to sound casual, as if chatting with a dirty old man's Japanese schoolgirl fetish is an everyday occurrence. Deliza throws some books into her locker, grabs another, and turns back to me. She leans in close. She whispers.

"Hey, Billy, you want to go out with me Friday night? I might even suck your dick."

My balls jerk as if cupped by a handful of ice cubes.

"You mind going on a skateboard?" I say.

"A skateboard," she says.

"It's how I roll," I say.

Deliza laughs. We both know there's no way we're ever going to hang together let alone engage in illicit sex acts. Even so, we're pretty good locker buddies. And we're not all that unalike. Deliza runs with the popular crowd, but the truth is, we both fly solo.

"You are one weird chavo, Billy."

Point of reference.

Chavo is this poor, homeless orphan in an old Mexican sitcom. The plot revolved around the idea that the other characters think it's hysterical to insult him, beat the crap out of him, and generally torture him. Needless to say, the show was a huge hit.

Deliza leans in again. "It's why I like you." The tip of her tongue lightly touches the inside of my ear, the concha, which is Spanish slang for vagina. My *pelotas*, which is Spanish for balls, jerk again.

Deliza smiles like the total innocent she isn't. She turns away. Farther down the hall some jocks give her some shit, hoping she'll give them the time of day. She blows them a kiss, gives them a perfectly manicured, French-tipped middle finger, and moves on. Anything male wipes its brow and begins to breathe again.

It's not even the highlight of the day.

10

Though most of the students at High School High leave campus for lunch, some of them even going home and not returning, the school still provides meals for people. The food is pretty much inedible but the old school cafeteria is pretty nice. It's usually a quiet place to read. In fact, a lot of people skip lunch and just use it as a study hall.

But today, maybe because it's still early in the year, it's a scene. It's noisy and almost crowded, people hanging out, each with their own tribe, jocks and queen bees at one table, the black athletes, nerds, aspiring rockers, emos punks, and surfers at others. Thankfully there's an empty table over by the window. I'm reading some sci-fi novel about some little kid who defeats a race of alien ants and saves the known universe. It's ridiculous but the only other book in my knapsack is *Being and Time*, by the philosopher Martin Heidegger, which is also ridiculous but it's the kind of ridiculous that takes a concentration and focus that is not especially conducive to cafeterias. So today it's alien ants.

"Hey, Billy. Can I sit?"

It's Ephraim and I don't look up. Ephraim Landgraf is my neighbor, meaning we live down the street from one another, each of us behind locked gates and high walls. Ephraim is small and skinny and, without his glasses, half blind. He has straw-colored hair that doesn't seem so much blond as lifeless. Ephraim's the kind of kid who gets pushed around for no real reason. The kind of kid, you play hide-and-seek, you don't look for him.

"It's not my chair," I say.

Ephraim sits and dives into the prepackaged, pre-servative-infested lunch he's brought from home. It's truly a magnificent collection of unhealthy, high-fat food groups. Ephraim is the kind of kid who would eat alien ants.

"I found Death Hunt 9," Ephraim says. This, coming out of nowhere.

Death Hunt 9 is a video game so violent it hasn't been released. The only way to get it is to illegally download a bootleg copy off the Net. Only the truly wounded would want this game and Ephraim's been searching for it for weeks.

"Good for you, Ephraim, now go disappear into your bedroom, and let me read about alien ants, okay?"

"Nah," says Ephraim. "I already beat it. It wasn't hard at all . . . no way . . . yeah . . ." His voice trails off. He sounds disappointed.

Here's the thing.

Ephraim surprised his parents. His siblings are all at least fifteen years older than he is and Ephraim's mother was never supposed to get pregnant again. Hence his parents have decided Ephraim didn't really happen and they ignore him. And because they do, Ephraim spends the majority of his time living as an avatar in an online, computer-based community in Illinois. The avatar is nothing like him. Ephraim's avatar has his own apartment, an important job, a social life. He, the avatar, even gets laid on occasion. Ephraim's built an online fantasy world where he's safe and happy and can control things. In real life, Ephraim stays home sick a lot.

"Hey! Hey, Willard!"

Ephraim and I both turn to see that a couple of tables away a big, handsome guy named John Montebello is standing, gesturing for someone to join him. On the moron scale of one to ten, John Montebello is a twenty. If Dad—*Gordon*—has decided he's earned everything we have, John Montebello has long since decided he's earned everything his father has.

"Hey, Willard, over here!"

Willard Twomey has come out of the kitchen, a tray in his hands. I've seen him in classes now, a couple of days running. He still hasn't uttered a word, still hasn't so much as *looked* at anyone. If he's changed his clothes since his first day of school, you wouldn't know it.

"Come on, dude!" says Montebello. "Sit with us!"

Montebello's at a table surrounded by his popular jock posse who, added up, push the moron scale into the high two hundreds. Normally they wouldn't be here at all. All of a sudden I wonder if they've planned this.

"C'mon, we don't bite! *Much!*"

Again, I get the sense that Willard Twomey feels none of this is happening to him, and if it is, he couldn't care less. Montebello nudges the kid right next to him out of his seat.

"Pull up a chair, dawg. You don't want to eat by yourself, right?"

Fact.

"Dawg" is an example of what is called Ebonics. Ebonics is the study of nonstandard African-American vernacular English, meaning speech often used by black people.

Sidebar.

The closest kids like John Montebello ever get to black people is listening to deafening rap music while parked at stoplights with the windows of the car rolled down.

Willard Twomey crosses to the table, sits down and begins to eat. Montebello looks around at his jock posse as if to say, Watch this.

"So, Willard. Monaghan got you up to speed yet? 'Cause, dude, you look like you still got the *brakes* on."

Har-har-har. The jocks all snark and slap palms with one another as if in the entire history of the world, this is the sharpest thing anyone has ever said.

Willard Twomey just eats his food.

"Willard, huh? That's, uh—that's kind of a retarded name, huh?"

Giggle-gaggle-gaw! Willard Twomey eats his food.

"Y'know, there was this movie called *Willard*. All about this freaky guy who loved rats. I mean, like, he *slept* with rats, Willard. When he took a dump in the morning, he did it with a freakin' rat on his lap. You do that? You take dumps with *rats*? Is that *cheese* you're eatin' or what, dawg?"

The jocks think that's *really* hysterical. One of them gags and spurts milk out his nose.

Willard Twomey eats.

"Yeah, ol' Willard here looks like a guy who loves his rat food," says Montebello. "Squeaky-squeak!"

"Squeaky-squeak," intone all the other morons at the table, in different voices, a regular rat choir. "Squeaky-squeak."

Wiping his mouth with the back of his hand, Willard Twomey rises. Montebello looks surprised, then annoyed. He's definitely not used to people his own age ignoring him, especially when he's being such a comedian.

"Hey, Willard, come again, when you can't stay so long, okay? And say hi to your rats."

Willard Twomey picks up his tray and swings it into John Montebello's head, knocking him out of his chair. Plate, silverware, and uneaten food fly.

No one can believe it. John Montebello began lifting weights at age twelve just to get a head start on beating people up. As Montebello tries to rise, Willard Twomey hits him over the head with the tray again and again, forcing him back down to the floor until he curls into a fetal position and covers up.

"Fuck!" Montebello whimpers. "Fuck!"

No one can believe it.

Willard Twomey throws the broken tray down at John Montebello. It bounces off his head and clatters away.

Believe it.

Willard Twomey turns. He stares contemptuously at the other jocks as if daring someone to do something. *Anything.* Not one of them moves, not even the guy with milk in his nose.

The dam breaks and the whole room begins hubbubbing at once. Some of the surfers are laughing. The Asian kids are talking excitedly in Chinese. The black guys are all slapping palms. Girls are pretending to be horrified. Faculty members come rushing across the cafeteria from wherever it is they've been standing. One goes to Montebello. Two others grab Willard Twomey who is as docile as a baby as he's led out.

I've never seen real violence before. I see why people find it effective.

"He's awesome," whispers Ephraim.

11

It's twenty minutes later and I'm moving down the hallway past the school office when I glance through the open door and see that Willard Twomey is sitting on a bench.

It's postbell but I'm in no real rush. After lunch it's fourth period calculus and I always take some time getting there because I know the teacher, Mr. Thurmond, is still in the faculty lounge sucking down his umpteenth cancer stick of the day.

Mr. Thurmond, who is heavy and sad faced, is an aspiring stand-up comedian who puts flyers of his open-mike nights on the classroom bulletin board, never realizing none of us are old enough to get in. He also uses the class to try out his material, which means he tries to make calculus funny. Calculus, which studies the limits, functions, derivatives, and integrals of numbers, is about as funny as an abscessed tooth and so is Mr. Thurmond.

"What did the zero say to the eight?" he'll say. "Nice belt!"

"What is the first derivative of a cow?" he'll says. "Prime rib."

No one laughs.

Which confuses and disappoints Mr. Thurmond. And makes him anxious. Which makes him want a cigarette. Which makes him excuse himself and run down the hall to the teacher's lounge. The class is pretty much Mr. Thurmond's only good joke.

I stop and look around to see if anyone is coming, and when I see that no one is, I turn back and go into the school office. Except for Willard Twomey and some secretary, there's nobody else there. I clear my throat. The secretary looks up from whatever it is she's doing. Unprepared for the port-wine hemangioma on my face, she flinches.

"Shouldn't you be in class?" she says. No hello, no may I help you.

"I need to see the nurse," I say.

"For what?" she says. She seems alarmed. Like maybe a birthmark is possibly contagious.

"For a brain tumor," I say.

Actually, I don't say that.

"My stomach hurts," I say. "I think I ate something at lunch." Which is true. It was something.

The secretary sighs as if she's besieged on a daily basis by disfigured people who have gotten sick from eating something at lunch and it's exhausted her.

"Have a seat," the secretary says. "I'll see if she's in."

She gets up and she leaves, probably down the hall to

join Mr. Thurmond and the school nurse in the faculty lounge for a quick smoke.

Willard Twomey is still sitting on the long wooden bench, acting as if I'm not even there. I go over and sit down next to him, leaving room between us. Now both of us are acting as if the other isn't there. I realize I can hear Mr. Esposito, the principal, talking on the phone in the inner office. He has a surprisingly strong, authoritative voice.

"Yes, I understand . . . No, but I do want to know who's responsible for him . . ."

Obviously he's talking about Willard Twomey.

"Very impressive," I say, not looking at Willard Twomey.

Willard Twomey doesn't say anything.

"What you did in the cafeteria today."

Willard Twomey doesn't so much as blink.

"Montebello's an idiot."

"What are you?" says Willard Twomey. He stares straight ahead. I notice that on the back of his right hand Willard Twomey has another tattoo.

Chaos.

And on the back of his left hand yet another.

Change.

". . . yes, well, I think we should have been informed that the young man has a juvenile record and a history of physical assault," says Principal Esposito in his surprisingly strong voice.

"Who's he talking to?" I say.

I don't think Willard Twomey is going to answer. But then he does.

"My grandmother. Like she's going to do anything but make herself another drink." Willard Twomey sounds disgusted.

"I understand. Yes, I'm sure it is difficult for you," says Principal Esposito's voice, full of authority.

I don't remember the last time I've done this. Maybe I never have. But I do now. I stick out my right hand.

Fact.

A handshake is a ritual in which two people grasp one another's hands. It is thought by some to have originated as a way of saying, There is no weapon in my hand. I'm not going to cut your head off. This, of course, is unless it's the left hand, which in many parts of the world is a way of saying, I'm going to use your head to wipe my ass.

"Billy Kinsey," I say.

Willard Twomey looks at my outstretched right hand. And now he looks at me. *At me.* Willard Twomey doesn't flinch, he doesn't waver. He *studies* my face. It is rude and disconcerting to the point of panic inducing and I have to force myself not to look away. His eyes trace the periphery of my right cheek and all of a sudden that side of my face begins to burn.

Point of reference.

Dorie used to say that my birthmark lightened or darkened, ebbed and flowed in shade and intensity, according to my emotions, and that a person could tell what

I was feeling just by looking at it. Which is just another reason why I always try to feel nothing at all.

Sidebar.

Dorie thought my port-wine hemangioma was beautiful.

Willard Twomey reaches out and lightly taps my open hand with a closed fist. "Twom," he whispers. He repeats himself, says it louder. "Twom Twomey."

"Not Willard?" I say. I make sure I sort of smile as I say it.

"Not unless you want a tray in your head." He's sort of smiling too. The tap with the fist, I decide, is an original way of saying, I'm not going to kill you *yet*.

"I look forward to meeting you as well," we hear Esposito's voice say. It sounds like he's wrapping things up which means it's time to get out of there. I stand.

"See you around," I say.

"I thought you were sick," says Twom Twomey.

"Miraculously cured," I say.

I beat it out of the office into the hall. When I look back I can see Esposito standing over Twom Twomey, lecturing. Twom Twomey, looking bored to stone, is staring at Mr. Esposito's navel. Esposito might as well be talking to the wall.

Twom. Twom as in "tomb." A mausoleum. A place for the dead. Dad thinks I should have a new friend. I wonder what he'll think about one who's now baptized my open palm with the right hand of *chaos*.

12

Don't walk in front of me, I may not follow. Don't walk behind me, I may not lead. Just walk beside me and be my friend.

So said Albert Camus, the French author and proponent of absurdism, who in 1960 died in a car accident along with his close friend Michel Gallimard, who was behind the wheel. At the last moment Camus had decided not to take the train. And when you figure that if Camus *had* been on the train and *not* beside his friend Michel Gallimard, he would have lived, this is about as absurd as it gets.

Absurd is how I've always pretty much felt about friendship.

I see guys who are supposed to be friends with each other and it's pretty much all jackass insults and look at the tits on her and let's get wasted. If you're Ephraim, it's computer-generated realities and chat rooms and online gaming portals. And let's not even talk about girls who go around in packs but will turn on one another at a moment's notice over not just a guy but a misplaced hairbrush. And let's say you do make a friend, all the research tells you that eventually they're probably going to move away or go to college or get a job someplace else or die even and you'll never see them again. So you'll move on and become friends with someone else and then someone else and as time goes by the bonds of friendship will get weaker and weaker until you're some drunk guy at a cocktail party trying to remember the names of people you're supposed to know. Like *Gordon.*

Still.

If absurdism is the desire for meaning in a world that doesn't have any, then perhaps friendship is as well.

I've decided it's worth a try.

I'm sitting, waiting on a bench, when Twom Twomey comes out and down the steps of High School High. Kids stare, then look away as they pass him. Everyone has heard what the new kid did. He ignores them and keeps going. He carries no books, no backpack. Like Mom and Dad, he shares similar physical characteristics with the locals but, as yet unassimilated, is a different animal altogether. And then he sees me looking at him. Twom stops and stares a moment and then walks over.

"What are *you* doing?" he says. As if me sitting there with nothing but a skateboard and a backpack for company is a pretty moron thing to do.

"I wanted to find out if you were suspended," I say Which is a moron thing to *say* because if he was suspended he wouldn't be standing there.

Twom sort of snorts. "They decided to give me a second

chance. Like I'm so grateful." I don't have to tell you he's being sarcastic.

We're both just standing there trying to think of something else to say when a car horn goes off and we both look out toward the street. A silver Porsche Boxster convertible, its top down, has pulled to the curb. John Montebello is behind the wheel. He leans on the horn again. The sound is more annoying than anything else. Chris Hardy, an offensive tackle, huge and stupid and a twenty-seven on the moron scale, is with him. Montebello rises in the seat. Arm outstretched, he points at Twom.

"You! Motherfucker! I'm going to find out where you fucking live! Because you are fucking dead! Look at me, fucker! It's the last fucking thing you will ever fucking see! Because you are so fucking, fucking dead!"

As if bored, Twom puts his thumb in his mouth. He moves it in and out. Meaning blow me. Montebello looks furious—then confused. Uncertain as to how to respond, he glares at me.

"You better watch your ass too, pie face!"

"Cool!" I call back. "Why don't I use your face as a mirror?"

Actually, I don't say that. But I do think it up later and wish I had.

Montebello revs the car's engine. He points at Twom again as if to say "you're it" and then jams the car in gear and starts to peel away. Only he stalls it completely. Thud—thump. And now when Montebello tries to start the car, the engine turns over but doesn't quite engage.

It tries to, it wants to, but it doesn't. Montebello, his expression semideranged, doesn't give it a break. He keeps the key turned in the ignition and he pumps the gas pedal up and down.

"Think you flooded it," says the ever brilliant Chris Hardy.

"Mother—*fucker!*" Montebello screams and he lashes out with his right arm, whacking Hardy in the head. Hardy cries out in pained surprise. Montebello swipes at him again, missing. Chris Hardy swipes back, also missing. They're like two pissed-off toddlers throwing elbows.

You couldn't rehearse it.

"Need a jump?" says Twom, making it sound as if he's concerned and would really like to be helpful to two idiots.

When Montebello goes to start the car this time, the engine grabs, falters, coughs, farts twice, and then finally engages. With a bleat of dark exhaust and sounding like a box of rocks, the car lurches away down the hill. Suddenly a skateboard doesn't seem half so stupid.

Twom turns back to me. He looks amused, as if he's been watching a good cartoon. He looks me up and down as if trying to decide whether or not I'm worthy.

I am. I know I am. I want to be.

"So what do you do for fun around this fucked-up place?" says Twom Twomey.

13

We go to Starbucks.

Fact.

Caffeine is a psychoactive stimulant and in certain plants is a natural pesticide that kills bugs. Taken in moderation, caffeine increases mental efficiency.

Sidebar.

On any given weekday afternoon, customers—mostly High School High students and mostly *girls*—are at Starbucks indulging in overpriced mochas, macchiatos, Frappuccinos, dolce lattes, white hot chocolates, and processed fruit smoothies, all of which have more sugar than coffee, have no nutritional value, cause weight gain, an imbalance in sex hormones, and possibly cancer. Little do they know that both caffeine and sugar can be ingested rectally. A good thing because I think Starbucks would frown on this.

"So where you from?" I say to Twom. We're sitting at a corner table. Twom is having black coffee and I'm having tap water.

"Why do you want to know?" Twom says.

"I don't. I'm just making conversation."

Twom laughs. "Cool." He dumps two sugars in his coffee. He stirs and sips. "Seattle. Like Starbucks."

"I hear it's nice."

"Someone is lying to you."

"Really?" I'm surprised. Seattle is the Emerald City. In what was Dorie's favorite book, L. Frank Baum's *The Wonderful Wizard of Oz*, the Emerald City is where the wonderful wizard lives. One just assumes he has any number of pleasant options.

"It rains. When it doesn't rain, it molds."

Oz, of course, is green not because it rains but because everyone wears green-tinted glasses. The movie doesn't tell you that. Movies don't tell you a lot of things.

We're interrupted by the sudden sound of laughter. Across the room, a teen girl squad is sitting around a table, straws in their Fraps, throwing glances in Twom's direction. When they see us looking they all immediately start pretending we're not there. All except Deliza Baraza. She's still sporting her sport geisha look, only now her blouse is unbuttoned halfway down to reveal a glimpse of lacy bra. Yeah, it's us, her eyes and her breasts say. What are you going to do about it?

"So you're staying with your grandmother?"

"Huh?" says Twom, his eyes never leaving Deliza.

"Your grandmother?"

"What about her?"

"You're, like, roommates or something?"

"Sort of, yeah. Got some major talent here, dude."

Meaning Deliza, who hasn't so much as blinked yet. It's a heavy-lidded stare-down, otherwise known as a human mating ritual.

"How come?"

"How come what?"

"How come your grandmother?"

Twom looks away from Deliza and at me. He sighs. "Okay, dude, it's like this. My folks are messed up, okay? They're fucking derelicts. The only reason they stay together is because nobody else would have them. Living with relatives is pretty much all I do. Okay?"

"Sounds tough." Which seems kind of an understatement.

"It's better than foster care. Anything else you want to know?"

"No," I say. "Anything *you* want to know?"

Twom gives me an amused look. "Surprise me." Meaning it's doubtful I could. And now, wouldn't you know it.

"Hey, Billy."

I look up and the day is complete. It's Ephraim again. He's approached the table and now he stands there, fidgeting, glancing at Twom, quickly glancing away.

"Ephraim," I say. Noncommittal. Meaning "go away."

Ephraim stares at the tabletop. At his feet. At his chewed-to-the-quick fingernails. For some reason I suddenly decide to be magnanimous. I hate feeling sorry for people. Even Ephraim.

"Twom, this is Ephraim. Ephraim—Twom."

Twom looks Ephraim up and down as if Ephraim might

be some weird species of skinny, featherless, sightless bird.

"How you doing, Ephraim?" he finally says.

"Hi, yeah, hi—good," says Ephraim, his eyes blinking rapidly. "I—I just wanted to say—what you did today—to Montebello—wow—that was—that was so sick."

"I'm glad you approve," Twom says.

"Oh, yeah, I do . . . yeah . . ." says Ephraim.

Twom looks back across the room to see that Deliza and her posse are all getting up and heading for the door. Deliza stops to stretch slightly, making her breasts pop. She throws a last lingering look back over her shoulder that's the visual equivalent of her tongue touching the inside of my ear. Twom's look back to her is pretty much the same thing only it's not Deliza's ear he's licking. You just know you're watching two certified professionals at work. And then she's gone.

"Hey, anybody need anything?" It's Ephraim, who's so oblivious to the whole boy-girl thing he might as well be from Pluto, which is no longer a planet. "On me," he says. "I'm loaded." In trying to show his cash, he drops it. When he bends to the floor to pick it up, he hits his head on the table. It's really a terrific whack.

"Sorry," he says. " It's okay, I'm all right."

It's pretty pathetic and it's definitely not all right but now Twom looks as if he feels sorry for him too.

"Sure," he says. "I'll have a donut, buddy."

Buddy. If Ephraim had a tail, he'd wag it. "Great! Yeah! Okay!" Ephraim turns to me. "Billy? On me?"

For the second time in five minutes, I'm feeling oddly benevolent. It seems like such an easy thing to do.

"Two."

"Cool!" says Ephraim. "I'll be right back . . . yeah!"

He turns and hurries toward the counter, thrilled to be of use. Two minutes later he's back with ten glazed, old-fashioned donuts. They're probably about fifty-seven thousand calories apiece and the crazy thing is, we eat all of them.

14

This is the day that as I move down the hall between classes, the tall, slim girl with the light red hair and the green eyes calls out to me again.

"Billy! Billy, hi!"

She stops as if she wants to talk to me but I ignore her and keep going.

"Billy?"

The side of my face feels like twisted, molten lead.

"Billy, it's *me*!"

I keep going as fast as I can.

"Billy!"

Maybe she'll think I'm someone else.

15

I find that Twom is full of surprises.

It's an afternoon about a week later and I'm on my skateboard heading home after school. I hear the odd purr of an engine coming up behind me. It's a BMW motorcycle, a big touring model, and it pulls to the curb in front of me. When the rider takes off his visored helmet and looks back, I see that it's Twom.

"Nice bike," I say. Not because I'm crazy about motorcycles but because it is.

"Yeah, not bad," Twom says. He reaches for the second helmet that's on the backrest. "Get on, I'll give you a ride home."

"How long you had it?" I say as I get on the bike.

"About four minutes," Twom says.

I quickly get off the bike.

"You stole it?"

"No. I borrowed it."

"From who?"

"I dunno."

"You *stole it* then."

"Dude. Stealing is when you keep things. Borrowing is when you bring them back."

I find this questionable logic at best and tell him so. Twom proceeds to inform me he is an experienced expert at "borrowing" motorized vehicles of just about any make and means and that he knows of what he speaks.

"What if you get caught?"

"You get arrested."

"Yes—*and?*"

"You spend the night in jail. Dude, it's no big deal." It's all part and parcel, Twom explains, of occasionally *going a little outlaw.* Going a little outlaw means—

"You don't let assholes dictate the rules."

Going a little outlaw means—

"*You* are your own authority. It's called *living,* dude. Something people oughta learn to *do* around here."

I accept Twom's offer of a ride. However, I make a mental note to jump off the bike, literally or figuratively, at a moment's notice.

I also soon discover that despite his revolutionary's attitude toward rules and authority, Twom has his own highly evolved sense of right or wrong. He dislikes what he calls the "dickhead club" and he has complete empathy for the underdog.

For example.

There's the fat girl. I don't even know her name. I don't think anybody does. She's one of those girls who goes around with her head down, hoping no one will notice her, and she succeeds at it. But you can tell by the end of the first week, she's totally, madly in love with Twom. She sort of plants herself in the right places, and when we pass her in the hall, she goes into some kind of fugue state. Her vision seems to blur, her mouth hangs open. She trembles. You can't help but notice. He puts up with this for about a week.

"Hey, how you doin'?" Twom says.

He's stopped and walked over to her. She stares at him, turning forty shades of crimson.

"What's your name?" Twom says.

She can barely get it out. "Ophelia," she says. It's a tough name to give an overweight, sweaty girl with badly cut, mousy blond hair.

"C'mon, I'll walk you to class, Ophelia."

And he does. He chats with her the whole way, asking her questions about herself. And after that, every time he sees her, he makes a big deal about saying hello and talking to her and walking with her. He'll even go over and sit with her while she's having lunch. She doesn't eat a bite. And it might be my imagination but, after a while, she doesn't seem nearly so heavy. Maybe even kind of cute.

Twom turns out to be an amazing athlete. We're in High School High's overcrowded, mandatory, biweekly phys-ed class one day, where half the students always loiter off to the side in their regular clothes, waiting for idiot time to be over, and all of a sudden, grabbing a football, he tells me to go long. And I don't know why, maybe because I want to impress him, I take off, running as fast as I can, which is actually pretty fast. Twom waits about ten seconds and then casually lets it go. It's on a string, at least thirty-five yards, a perfect buzzing spiral, and it hits me in the hands, just about breaking them or at least that's what it feels like. They go totally numb. But somehow I hold on. And it's stupid but I'm really pleased that I do. I'm pleased that he's thrown this bullet of a pass and that I've caught it.

"Brutha!" yells Twom.

Twom can run like a track star, can dunk a basketball, and can probably throw a baseball through a wall while walking on his hands. It's only a matter of weeks before every coach at High School High is asking him to come out for their team. Twom just laughs at them. "Dickhead club," he says later. "Like *that's* ever gonna happen." He pretends he's toking on a joint.

One thing Twom doesn't do very well is schoolwork. Which is odd because most of the time he seems like a pretty bright guy. But then one day Mr. Monaghan asks him to read a paragraph out loud in class and Twom suddenly looks like someone's asked him to jump off a steep cliff. He quietly refuses in a way . . .

"I don't think so."

. . . that says if even slightly pushed, it all might get ugly very quickly for Mr. Monaghan.

"Let's talk about it after class," says Mr. Monaghan, nervously. But Twom doesn't stay.

When I ask him about it later, he just shrugs.

"I don't read good, dude. The letters don't look right."

Point of reference.

Dyslexia or developmental reading disorder is when the brain doesn't recognize certain information. It has nothing to do with the ability to think or understand ideas.

"No big deal," Twom says. "I'm just in school till they throw me out."

"Then what?"

"Then I join the rest of the bottom feeders."

It makes you realize how so much of standardized education just completely sucks. It's all about what educators think they should stick in your head so you'll be a so-called productive member of society, and if it doesn't stick, even if it's not your fault, you're written off as a failure. And then, you pretty much begin to think of yourself as one.

I start doing Twom's homework for him. I write essays for him to turn in. I summarize reading assignments and lectures so he can understand them. One day he even raises his hand in class. He gives the right answer, sending shock waves through the room. We get a surprise quiz and I slip him the answers. I partner with him in chemistry and we get an A on a lab experiment. We're the only ones that do, and because people have no reason to think of me as the brightest bulb in the lamp, Twom gets all the credit.

Much to my surprise, it's sort of fun, not holding back. And even though we both pretend to think it's hysterical, Twom is sort of thrilled. And I'm not used to helping people and find it's not an unacceptable feeling.

What's not so funny is that after years of trying to avoid him, I've suddenly inherited Ephraim.

Unlike Ophelia, he doesn't stay in one place, waiting. He constantly follows us, tagging along behind. Twom doesn't encourage him. If he does an Ephraim thing, like walk into an open door and knock himself senseless, Twom won't wait up for him. But if he gets himself up off the floor and catches up to us, Twom won't tell him to go away.

Twom and I go into the showers after gym class one day just in time to see Chris Hardy push Ephraim out of the way so he can take his shower. Ephraim, who is nearly blind without his glasses, slips on the wet floor and falls. His head hits the floor. Twom goes over and helps him up.

"You okay, buddy?"

Ephraim nods. They're both naked and Ephraim looks surprised and embarrassed at the physical contact. And now Twom turns to Hardy, whose eyes are closed under the spray. Hardy is huge from weight lifting. There are pimples all over his shoulders and back, even his ass.

Reaching out with one hand, Twom grabs Hardy by the cock and balls. Hardy screams and tries to jerk away, which is a mistake because Twom has his nuts in a death grip.

"You like pushing people around?"

Hardy just screams some more. Everybody's watching. The vast majority of kids in the shower room have never touched anyone's dick but their own and I'm sure they'd all now agree that it seems a good way to put a guy on the defensive. Ephraim's eyes are like saucers.

"What are you, a faggot!?" screams Hardy.

"You tell me, after I shove it up your ass," says Twom, squeezing hard enough to make Hardy bellow again. All the younger kids shudder. The thought of an erect dick going anywhere *near them* is terrifying. Twom finally lets go of Hardy and shakes his hand as if there's something funky on it.

"Play nice from now on. Especially with my friends."

You can tell Hardy wants to throw a punch but he's in too much pain. Cupping his balls and groaning, he hightails it out. Twom gives Ephraim back his shower. He turns to wait for one of his own. Needless to say he's now the hero of every kid in the locker room, especially Ephraim who now has heard the unhoped-for magic word. No one has ever called him a friend before.

He talks about the event for days.

16

It's a Monday study period and I'm in the school library where nobody ever goes, surrounded by books that nobody ever reads. I like the library. I like thinking that *I'm* a book nobody ever reads. I'm still trying to get through *Being and Time,* which is proving to be one tough nut to crack. All it seems to be saying is that life is a bitch and then you die, and frankly, it seems pointless to write an entire treatise trying to prove something that any moron could tell you is true without thinking twice. I'm just about ready to pack ol' Martin Heidegger in for good when somebody sits down across from me. When I look up I see it's the girl with the light red hair and green eyes and my stomach lurches.

Fact.

Red hair is a genetic mutation. Less than four percent of the world has red hair, and by 2050, geneticists predict that because of global intermingling, it will be practically nonexistent.

Sidebar.

Red is the color of blood and fire. The Greek philosopher Aristotle believed that redheads were emotionally unhousebroken. Redheads are sensitive to physical pain.

The girl with the light red hair and green eyes stares at me. She didn't have to tell me the first time that her name is Gretchen Quinn.

"Have I done something to offend you?" Gretchen Quinn says.

"No," I say. At least I think I say that. My mind is not quite sure if my mouth is talking.

"Am I stupid?" Gretchen says. "Ugly?"

"No." She isn't. Not even a little bit.

"So why do you act like you don't even know me? Dorie was my best friend. I thought you were my friend too, Billy."

"I don't really know you anymore," I say. It's a totally moron thing to blurt out, but spur of the moment, it's the best I can do. Gretchen Quinn stares at me. She quietly nods. She rises and moves away from the table. She leaves the library as quietly as she came in. The side of my face is freezing cold.

Point of reference.

Dorie and Gretchen met in the second grade and from that moment on were pretty much inseparable. There was this old bedtime story Dorie and I had read as kids about two sisters, Snow White and Rose Red, who were crazy about each other and did everything together and that's what I'd call them. Dorie was Snowy and Gretchen was Rosy. Rose Red was chatty and cheerful and Snow

White was quiet and thoughtful and that sort of suited them too. In the fairy tale Rose Red and Snow White had this bear that would come and visit them. And they'd ride him like a pony and pull his fur and tie his feet together and then tickle him. And the bear would yell out, "Snowy-White and Rosy-Red! Will you beat your lover dead?"

A lot of times I'd pretend to be the bear.

The other thing about Snow White and Rose Red is they promised they'd never leave each other. That didn't happen. Dorie—*Snowy*—died.

Gretchen and I didn't see each other much after that. I sort of had to take a little time off, and then after that, I got stuck in the special, big-deal middle school before ultimately bailing on it. In the meantime, Gretchen's father, who was a hotshot doctor of infectious diseases, took the entire family off to Africa so they could save people who were dying of AIDS and whatnot. So she really was gone. But now, she had said it all that day on the beach. "We're back."

It goes without saying that girls make you do insane things. One minute a guy can be, if there is such a thing, *normal*, the next, he's cracking stupid jokes and running and dancing in place like a babbling, mindless idiot. Another word for this is "dating."

This had to be immediately nipped in the bud.

17

"Your parents ever let you out of the house?"

It's later in the day between classes and Gretchen Quinn is at her locker. If she's surprised to see me standing there, she doesn't show it.

"No, they keep me in a cage in my room," Gretchen says.

This is called "flirting." Flirting often precedes dating and is an equally sinister endeavor.

"To do what?" Gretchen says.

"How about I drag you to a deserted cabin in the dark woods and do a vivisection with a chain saw?"

Actually, I don't say that. In all honesty, it freaks me out that I even think it.

"The movies?" I say. I sort of shrug. I hate the movies. Vivisections with chain saws are the basis of a lot of movies.

"They'd want to meet you," Gretchen says. "My parents."

"They have already," I say.

"They'd want to meet you again," Gretchen says.

"Why?" I say. "To see if they can still trust me?"

"They're funny that way."

The side of my face begins to feel warm, but it's not unpleasant. "How do you know *you* can trust me?" I say.

"I just do," Gretchen says.

Fact.

Leonardo da Vinci's *Mona Lisa* is believed to have been painted between 1503 and 1506. The ambiguity of her expression is often described as mysterious.

Not anymore.

Looking at Gretchen Quinn, the stain on my face just about *glowing*, I know, without a doubt, what Mona Lisa was smiling about.

Me.

18

From having been there before, I know that Gretchen and her family live in this old-fashioned, Craftsman-style house that looks as if it was actually built with materials and colors that in all probability exist in nature. It's not really superhuge but, still, it sits on almost a half acre of land, which is pretty much unheard of in High School Highville. Inside it's open and clean with hardwood floors and throw rugs and shelves with books and walls with framed children's drawings. There's a living room that looks like people sit in it as opposed to visit it on rare occasions. There's even a fireplace that has the remains of actual wood logs in the grate.

I like it.

Gretchen's parents are in the kitchen and they immediately jump to their feet, all smiles, as if they're happy to see me. They don't seem to have changed much or gotten any older even though I'm sure they have. Dr. Quinn—*Jim*—is still this guy who you can tell was a terrific athlete when he was young. He probably made about a million baskets and led his team to the state championship before going on to college and then medical school, where he no doubt graduated first in his class. And now he gets up every morning and runs five miles without fail, does pushups and calls it quality time. He's the one Gretchen gets her red hair and green eyes from. Mrs. Quinn— *Kath*—is the sort of no-nonsense woman who's smart and organized as hell, and you just know she was the one who decorated the house and that she has a ton on the ball because not only was she once a big-deal hospital administrator, she also landed Dr. Quinn, who was a catch.

Don't tell me all people are created equal because they're not.

Dr. Quinn crushes my hand and Mrs. Quinn gives me a smile and asks what I've been up to.

"Not much," I say.

"A senior," says Mrs. Quinn. "Any plans for next fall?"

"Not really," I say.

"How are those folks of yours?" says Dr. Quinn.

"How are they supposed to be?" I say, wrinkling my brow as if I don't quite understand the question. I'm coming off like a real ignoramus. At least I hope I am. My problem is I like the Quinns. This might be seeping through and so I make a point of being especially rude as we leave.

"You two be careful," says Mrs. Quinn.

"We're just going to do drugs with used needles and have unprotected sex," I say.

Actually, I don't have the balls to say that.

"We'll try," I say.

"And have a good time," says Dr. Quinn.

"As opposed to what?" I say.

It's just starting to get dark when Gretchen and I come out. Gretchen is starting to look a little uncertain. So far, so good.

"Listen, there's something you should know," I say.

"What?" she says.

"I don't drive," I say.

"Oh. Well, I could probably get the car," Gretchen says. She doesn't sound too sure.

"No, it's covered," I say.

I point and Gretchen turns to see the old hulk of a Cadillac parked at the entrance of the Quinn driveway. It's like something out of an Elvis Presley in his grilled-peanut-butter-and-banana-sandwiches period—a faded beast with pointed fins, rusting chrome, stained white-wall tires, and a grille that looks like a bum with several teeth knocked out. The chauffeur is waiting by the rear door, grinning like a bloodthirsty fiend.

Twom.

"He offered to drive," I say.

Gretchen sort of slowly nods. "Okay," she finally says.

I make the introductions.

"Little Red," says Twom, looking as if he could eat her. Gretchen is polite but it's tough. It's not so much the tattoos, spikes, and hoops, which are actually sort of *normal* these days, it's the wild eyes and the deranged, high-octane grin. With a bow and a big sweep of his arm, Twom opens the rear door of the Cadillac.

"Your chariot awakes," he says. Gretchen quickly slips in past him.

"Awaits," I say.

"Huh?"

"Not wakes—*waits*."

"Get your ass in there, dude," Twom says, "before I do." I can tell he's more than a little impressed with Gretchen, and for some weird reason, I feel annoyed about it. The car, which belongs to Twom's grandmother, smells of dogs, pine freshener, cigarette smoke, and molding leather. There's dog hair and bits of crumbled kibble on the seats and floorboards. Gretchen's hands are tight in her lap and her knees are up and together as if she's trying not to touch anything.

It's really perfect.

Twom gets in the front, slams the door behind him with a crash, and ignoring his seat belt, starts the car. Elvis turns over, falters, starts again, and with a billow of blue exhaust, settles into a deep, ragged thrum. Twom turns the radio on.

"How about some tunes!" he yells.

It's a crazed speed metal station and he turns it up full blast. The song, if you can call it that, sounds like someone whipping a horse to death. It makes further conversation all but impossible and is a totally terrific choice for the occasion.

Twom puts the Caddy in gear and we back up and out of the driveway. There's a horrible grinding sound as the undercarriage of the car hits the street.

"Next stop, AMC12!" Twom screams over the sound of the radio.

The evening can't get any better. I'm counting on it.

19

In 1891, Thomas Edison, the so-called inventor of the lightbulb, designed and patented the Kinetoscope. This was a simple box device that was the predecessor to all film projectors.

Better he should have electrocuted himself with his fluoroscope.

Exploding cars bear down on me. Exploding planes immolate in front of me. Exploding, bullet-riddled people scream and show their insides. And we haven't even gotten through the coming attractions yet. I look around and, much to my dismay, see nothing but enraptured faces.

What *is* good, though, is that Gretchen looks as awkward as I feel. This is because on the other side of Gretchen, Twom and Deliza Baraza are sitting together, heads close, whispering and giggling about something. By sheer luck, the evening has turned into a double date. In fact, it's a double date plus one because on the other side of Deliza and Twom sits a forlorn-looking, totally ignored Ephraim.

It happens like this.

Gretchen, Twom, and I are in the refreshment line,

buying popcorn with artificial butter that will probably cause stomach tumors, when someone calls my name.

"Billy!"

I turn to see that Deliza has entered the lobby with a group of well-dressed Latinas. They stop and hold back as she comes over to us. Deliza's wearing riding boots, cream-colored jeans, a tight T-shirt, and a butter-soft leather jacket. As usual, she's carrying about half a ton of self-assurance.

"You got your skateboard?" she says to me.

"It's parked outside," I say.

Across the lobby, one of Deliza's friends calls out in Spanish. Having taken four years of high school Spanish, which means I haven't actually learned to *speak* any Spanish, I think it translates as something like . . .

"Deliza, come on, we told Paco we'd save seats."

Deliza replies, saying something along the lines of . . .

"You want a seat, go sit on Paco's face!"

She turns back to us. "Slum night with the *cateto* side of the family," she says. *Cateto* means peasant.

"Hi, Deliza," says Gretchen.

Deliza turns and regards Gretchen a moment. "Hey," she finally says, as if it's an effort. I realize that she considers Gretchen a rival, and for some odd reason, I'm pleased that she does. Deliza turns now and stares at Twom, full bore. Twom is staring back.

"Gonna do the honors, Billy?"

"Twom, Deliza. Deliza, Twom." Not that this is news.

"So you're the guy," says Deliza, "who spanked John
Montebello's ass."

"What if I am?" Twom says.

"You gonna spank mine?"

"You want popcorn first?"

"You gonna butter it?"

"Salt it too."

It doesn't seem to be popcorn they're talking about.
And then, all of a sudden, wouldn't you know it—

"Hey! Hey, guys, hey!"

Ephraim approaches across the lobby at a half run, so
excited, he's like a baby giraffe about to trip over his own
feet.

"I didn't know you were going to the movies! Cool!
Way cool!" He's so loud and daffy sounding, it's beyond
excruciating. "Hey! Hey! We can all, like, sit together!"

Fate.

The great thing about fate is you can blame it for absolutely everything.

20

Whoo-whoo-whoo-whoo-whoo!

The movie is a second remake of *The Three Stooges*, and despite me wondering why we ever needed a first one, everyone thinks it's hysterical. The movie star moron playing one Stooge runs in circles, barks like a dog, and then pisses on a fire hydrant. The "comedian" playing the second Stooge hits him in the head with a hammer and then rips out handfuls of the third Stooge's hair. It's beyond terrible and I feel like I'm being swallowed by my seat. I'm also sort of dismayed that Gretchen seems to be enjoying it as this would mean the evening might be taking a positive turn.

It doesn't.

A little more than an hour later, Gretchen and I are standing on a sidewalk watching Twom get handcuffed by the police.

It goes like this.

The movie is finally over and we join the masses heading to the parking lot. Exit polls will later tell us, in

case we're not sure, that the two hours with the Three
Stooges has been time well spent. This is bad news because it will probably encourage the movie studio to make
yet another sequel. Frankly they'd do better to make and
market propofol, which is an operating room anesthetic.
Both put you to sleep but propofal erases the memories.

It seems obvious from the way Deliza is draped
around Twom she has no intention of letting the evening
end anytime soon. This is sadly derailed when her girlfriends approach to tell her that Paco of the seated face
was a no-show and they need rides home. Deliza looks
totally pissed but apparently she has no choice. She piles
her raven-haired *hermanas* into a four-door Mercedes sedan that looks half street rocket, blows Twom a heavy-
eyed kiss, and leaves. Ephraim, sorry to say, has already
been picked up by his mother, who has totally humiliated
everyone by screaming across the parking lot like an impatient Cruella de Vil nailing a Dalmatian—

"Ephraaaaim! Now!"

Five minutes later Twom, Gretchen, and I are in the
old Cadillac, driving down High School High Boulevard.
Twom keeps glancing in the rearview mirror as if waiting for me to jump Gretchen's bones full bore.

"Don't mind me!" He whistles tunelessly to himself.
"Not even here. Wheaka-wheaka-wheak!" He pretends
he's rolling up a screen between the front and back seats
so as to give us privacy. It's a great thing to do because it's
really discomforting.

"You're looking discomforted," I say to Gretchen. *Actually I don't say this.* But I encourage it by trying to look discomforted myself.

"Anybody want to go to In-N-Out Burger?" Twom says. Antibiotic-laden, hormone-injected beef. Great idea.

"I'm a vegetarian," Gretchen says.

The evening is now as good as over. But just as I'm about to suggest we call it a night and go home, Twom begins to sing. "In and Out! In and Out! That's what a first date's! All about!" Needless to say he makes it sound like fucking.

Gretchen doesn't so much as giggle.

She belly-laughs. "Stop," she says in a way that lets you know he shouldn't. She doesn't mind the innuendo, she thinks it's funny, thinks Twom is funny. And it hits me all at once that the reason she thinks it's funny is because it *is*. Twom is. He's been relaxed and funny all evening long. Gretchen is having a good time. *Has* been having a good time. The only one who's not, who hasn't been, who has been uncomfortable and nervous and so assumes everyone else is, is me. It is I who am the stooge.

Whoo-whoo-whoo-whoo-whoo!

That's when the siren goes off.

Twom pulls over. The police car, its lights flashing, pulls to the curb behind us. A policeman approaches and asks for a license and registration. Twom hands him a ticket stub from the AMC12. "This car belong to you?" asks the cop. You can tell he already knows the answer.

"It's my grandmother's," says Twom.

"Your grandmother has reported it as stolen."

"My grandmother can't find her teeth most mornings."

"She says your driver's license was suspended."

"That doesn't mean I don't know how to *drive*, dude."

The policeman tells all of us to get out of the car and we do. Twom is asked to assume the position. This means putting his hands on the hood of the car and spreading his legs. The policeman pats him down.

"Touch me there, you'll have to marry me," says Twom.

"I love smart guys," says the policeman.

"You must hate looking in the mirror," says Twom.

The policeman turns to Gretchen and me. He's not too old, maybe in his twenties. He's big, with buzzed blond hair. He looks like he wears his aviator sunglasses to bed at night.

"I hope *you two* have identification."

Gretchen quickly hands him her driver's license. He looks at it. He hands it back to her. You can tell by the way he does it, he thinks he's hot shit and she should think so too. I hand him my picture ID.

"What's this?"

"It's called a library card?"

Twom laughs like that's the funniest thing he's ever heard. "No wonder he doesn't know what it is!"

The policeman handcuffs him. If he's concerned, Twom doesn't show it. "See you, Little Red!" he says, all smiles, as he's pushed into the back of the police car.

The policeman closes the door and, adjusting his belt, turns back to us. His holstered gun looks like a block of metal on his hip. Like the Taylors', I'm pretty sure it's a Glock.

"You two need a ride?" he says, sounding bored now at the prospect.

"She's called her dad," I say.

"Let's be careful who we drive with next time," he says.

"You mean her dad?" I say.

The policeman gives me a look. He shakes his head at Gretchen as if he pities who she's stuck with. He turns and gets in the cruiser. His partner already has it started up and the two of them pull away. In the backseat Twom looks like he's whistling again.

And then they're gone.

The only thing that could make the evening more of a disaster now would be getting mugged, which is sort of what happens next.

Gretchen has turned, moved to the car, and is resting now against the rear bumper. I join her. We sit there for a while in silence.

"You know, I've been asking around," Gretchen says, not really looking at me.

"About what?" I say.

"You," Gretchen says softly.

"Really. What have you found out?" I'm not so much curious as I am alarmed.

"People don't know what to make of you. Some people think you're kind of cool. Most of them aren't sure. A couple of girls think you're going to come to school someday and shoot people."

"I'm not," I say.

"I know," says Gretchen. "Still . . . I feel like I should worry about you, Billy."

I know that her eyes are green and in the light of the street lamp I can see, or maybe it's just that I can imagine, a single tear running down her cheek.

It's just not fair.

Norepinephrine, phenylhydrazine, and dopamine, which act like amphetamines, hit my brain's pleasure center like a locomotive. My pupils dilate. My heart pumps faster. The chemical oxytocin floods my body, creating intense feelings of caring, attraction, and warmth. Physical contact produces endorphins and continued high doses of oxytocin. These chemicals are all natural opiates that create a druglike dependency.

Translation?

I am so screwed.

I lean toward her. Closing her eyes, Gretchen leans ever so slightly toward me. I kiss her. Her lips are the softest thing I've ever felt. I lean into her and her body presses against me. I gasp and almost pull away as her fingertips caress my right cheek.

"Sorry," says Gretchen quickly.

"No," I say. "It's okay."

And it is. Her touch is delicate and beneath it, as if under a special wavelength of light, I feel my cheek taking on vivid hues. We kiss again. Her tongue touches my lips—

And then a car horn blares and blows the moment right out of the water. We move away from each other, startled. We squint at the headlights of the van as it pulls up and then moves to the side of us. The passenger-side window glides down.

"Let's go, you two!" calls Gretchen's dad. He sounds like a cheerful friar who's come to deliver a chastity belt.

I wonder if Gretchen's going to get into the front but she doesn't. She climbs into the backseat with me. As we pull away, I turn and look over my shoulder. The Caddy looks like a tired beggar, alone under the streetlight. I wonder if anyone thought to lock it.

Even though he's been pulled out of his house at, like, ten-thirty at night, and even though he's seen me lip-locked with his daughter, Dr. Quinn doesn't seem especially upset. "Well. Other than the police, did you two have a pleasant evening?" He glances in the rearview to see if anyone is smiling at his joke. Or maybe, like Twom, he's waiting to see if I'm going to jump his "Little Red."

"Dad," Gretchen says. Which is a polite way of saying, Please don't embarrass me any more than you already have. At least Dr. Quinn doesn't have the radio going. You just know that, like Gordon, he's the kind of guy who likes classic rock and listening to Boston or Steely Dan or, even worse, Aerosmith, something I can't handle under the best of circumstances, let alone tonight.

"Boy, I feel like a regular chauffeur here," Dr. Quinn says now, all cheerful about it.

Again, it's one of those things that parents say when they want to let you know that they, too, were once young and went through all the same crap you're going through, and because they did, they can relate. And it's the last thing you want to hear because if they were once just like you, that means someday you're going to be just like them.

Just another thing to look forward to.

When they drop me off, Gretchen gets out of the car with me. "Call me, okay?" she says.

"I will." I even repeat it. "I will."

Gretchen gets in the front next to her dad. As they motor off, she opens the window, leans out to look back at me and waves. Before I can catch myself, I wave back. I don't so much as move until well after they're gone.

21

The vial of Ambien CR is on the second shelf of the cupboard to the left of the bathroom sink.

Ambien, like all sleep medications, is addictive and can cause memory loss and withdrawal symptoms. Prolonged use can also cause changes in behavior such as risk taking and decreased inhibitions.

I unscrew the safety lid and drop a couple of them into my hand. The pills are 6.25 milligrams and are round and a pinkish orange. I flush them down the toilet so that if she checks, Mom will think I'm using them.

It's when I'm in the bedroom undressing that I'm aware of someone coming out of the closet behind me. I look into the bureau mirror and I catch a glimpse of a hospital gown and an enormous syringe.

"This is going to hurt," Dorie says. She thrusts the needle into the base of my spine and I scream.

I jerk up in bed, flailing at the sheets.

Fact.

Dreams are neurons firing from the brain stem while the brain is undergoing memory consolidation during sleep. A recurring dream is a dream that is experienced repeatedly over a long period of time.

You'd think I'd recognize this one by now. You'd think I'd be able to remind myself what it is while I'm in the middle of it. But I'm not. I never have been. And now, like always, the room seems to be inhabited by shadows and barely concealed horrors. A sheet of sandpaper drags across my brain. It hits me that maybe the date with Gretchen was a dream as well.

I get out of bed and I begin pulling on clothes.

In the kitchen I drag open the drawer where the keys are. I head for the door. I think I might be crying.

Outside, I start to run. I don't know why. I've just got to get away from the house where Dorie's ghost still lives and constantly reminds me that I failed her. With nowhere else to go, I run up and across the street to the Taylors' empty morgue of a house. As I pass it, I kick the newspaper into the bushes.

I enter and shut the door behind me. I turn off the security alarm. The outside floods make it just light enough inside for me to see. I stand there, shivering in the air-conditioning. It takes a while but the fear finally begins to fade.

I make my way through the living room and up the stairs of the Taylors' house. I'm so tired, I can hardly put one foot in front of the other.

I enter the Taylors' bedroom. I look around. I look at the bed. I move to the bed. I touch the bed. It's soft. The house is quiet. I sit on the bed. And then I lie down on the bed. I can rest here. For some unexplainable reason, there are no nightmares in this house, and if there are, they're not mine. Dorie won't come here. It's safe here. I'm not sure when my eyes close. All I know is that I sleep.

22

When I wake up, the Taylors' dachshund is stupidly staring me in the face. He whimpers, shimmies on his belly across the bed and licks me on the lips. It hits me he's probably used to kissing Mrs. Taylor in the morning, maybe slipping her a little tongue, and the thought is so gross, it makes me roughly push him away.

It's at that very moment I hear the sound of the front door opening downstairs. I realize I forgot to reset the security system. I hear voices.

"Of all the goddamn . . ." says Mr. Taylor.

"Stop. Linda just must have forgotten," Mrs. Taylor says.

I hear them move into the living room, Mr. Taylor grumbling as he goes.

"Hey, it's just me!" I call. "Your neighbor, Billy Kinsey! I accidentally spent the night!"

I say absolutely no such thing.

My teenage brain goes into panic mode. Logic goes totally out the window. I desperately look around the room for any kind of help.

"Animals," intones the Taylors' dachshund, making itself comfortable on the bed, "respond to threats in different ways. Most will try to escape when threatened."

I get up and move to the sliding doors that face out onto the deck. The jump from the deck down to the poolside pavement is too much and I'm afraid to risk opening the doors anyway. I can hear the Taylors' luggage clunking as they start up the stairs.

"Maybe it was the maid," says Mrs. Taylor.

"Fucking idiot," says Mr. Taylor. I'm not sure if he's talking about Mom, Mrs. Taylor, or the maid. Maybe all three. Maybe women in general.

"Failing a means of escape," the Taylors' dachshund now tells me, "most animals will seek refuge. We will attempt to blend into our surroundings."

When Mr. Taylor opens the bedroom door, he sees nothing. Five minutes later he and Mrs. Taylor are unpacking. Mrs. Taylor opens the closet to put clothes away. She gasps in fright. I'm standing there hiding behind her designer clothes. They reek of Mrs. Taylor's perfume. Mrs. Taylor looks puzzled.

"Billy?" she says.

Of course, this doesn't happen. This would be embarrassing.

"Fear," warns the Taylors' dachshund, "makes an animal capable of anything."

I move to the bureau. I open the drawer as quietly as I can but still it creaks. Out in the hall it's suddenly silent.

"Is someone here?" I hear Mrs. Taylor say.

"Shhh," says Mr. Taylor.

"Maybe we should call the police," says Mrs. Taylor.

"Be quiet," says Mr. Taylor.

I reach into the bureau drawer for the gun. I can see it all so clearly. Mr. Taylor is opening the door to his son's bedroom. Robby Taylor is a senior at UC Santa Barbara majoring in drinking and is an asshole. Mr. Taylor grabs a baseball bat and turns back into the hallway.

"Tom, just call the police—"

Holding the gun now, I turn toward the closed bedroom door.

"Anything," repeats the Taylors' dachshund.

Mrs. Taylor screams as Mr. Taylor throws open the bedroom door and, bat raised, comes running in. I shoot him in the face. The gun is deafening. Blood and brains spatter the wall. Mrs. Taylor screams again. And then with a shock, she realizes it's me.

"Billy?" she says.

I blow Mrs. Taylor away.

Of course, this doesn't happen. This is a youthful imagination twisted and distorted by the soulless idiocy that is movies and television.

The Taylors' dachshund sighs with impatience. "With no place to run and no place to hide," it says, "an animal freezes and hopes for the best."

I'm just standing there when Mr. Taylor opens the door, charges in and, screaming, brains me with the baseball bat. I hit the floor like a sack of grain. I lie there. I can feel blood beginning to pool beneath my head. I'm vaguely aware of Mr. and Mrs. Taylor looking down at me.

"Billy?" says Mrs. Taylor.

Fortunately another option presented itself.

"Tom!" screams a terrified Mrs. Taylor as Mr. Taylor comes rushing in with nothing in his hands. He stops in surprise. Mrs. Taylor sticks her head into the room, behind him.

I'm holding the dachshund in my arms. The gun is in the bureau drawer. I'm trying to look as if I have no idea what's going on.

"Billy?" says Mrs. Taylor.

"Hi. You're home," I say. "I came over to feed, y'know, *the dog?*"

Twenty minutes later, I'm back at my house, sitting at the kitchen table, a bowl of cold cereal in front of me. Far from being suspicious, the Taylors have been ridiculously grateful. Mr. Taylor has even given me twenty bucks "to say thanks." I should probably have told him that there was a time when neighbors did things for one another for free, that it never occurred to them that they were going to get rewarded for helping out, that everyone was in it together and that they had to be to survive. But frankly, I wasn't around at that time so I took the money.

"Billy?"

Somewhere someone is talking.

"Billy!"

I look up. The someone is Mom.

"Huh?" I say.

"I said, did you have a good time last night?"

For a moment I think she's talking about the Taylors.

"What do you mean?"

"Gretchen," Mom says. "Did you have a nice time with Gretchen?"

Oh.

"It was okay," I say. "We went to the movies."

"Has she changed much?" says Mom.

"She's older," I say.

"Well, I know that," says Mom.

"She's still nice," I say.

"I'm sure she's lovely," Mom says.

Suddenly, and I'm not sure she even knows it, Mom looks sad and faraway. It suddenly makes me wonder if she has dreams of Dorie too. Mom catches herself. She tries to make herself look happy. She's not as good at it as I am.

"You'll have to have her come over sometime."

"Sure," I say.

I finish my cereal, hardly tasting. I'm thinking about last night. I'm thinking about this morning. I'm thinking I'm not sure if there is a word that adequately describes what sleep is to an insomniac. Release? Relief? Liberation? Mostly I'm thinking it might be time to go a little outlaw.

23

When Gretchen comes out of her first period class, I pretend I'm not there waiting for her. I just *happen* to be there as if studying strange linoleum is something I do on a daily if not hourly basis. Gretchen, of course, is talking to other girls. Girls always are talking to other girls. When she sees me, though, Gretchen stops and comes right over. She seems happy to see me. Which is pretty great because frankly I'm so glad to see her it's all I can do not to roll over on my back and pee on my belly like the Taylors' dachshund.

"Hey," Gretchen says.

"Hey."

We're both scintillating conversationalists.

"I thought you were going to call."

"You know how I don't have a driver's license?" I say. "Well, I don't have a phone either."

"Maybe you ought to do something about that," says Gretchen. Which is also pretty great because what she's saying is if I had a phone and I called her, yes, she'd answer every time.

I'm starting to feel a little calmer.

"I thought I could walk with you to class or something," I say. Because we're just standing there.

"Okay," Gretchen says, and we turn and walk.

All of about twenty-five feet.

"Well, here we are," says Gretchen, stopping.

"Whoa. Pretty convenient," I say. Which it is but not necessarily for me. We stand there for a moment, not really looking at one another. It feels like everyone who passes is staring at us. It's not a feeling I'm entirely crazy about.

"I was thinking we could hang out together again," I say. Actually I don't say it, I just sort of breathlessly blurt it. *"Iwasthinkingwecouldhangouttogetheragain."*

"I'd love to," says Gretchen. Which, when you get right down to it, is really the perfect thing to say.

"What do you like to do?" I say.

"Anything," Gretchen says.

"That makes it easy." Gretchen giggles and all of a sudden I'm feeling sort of confident. It's a nice feeling and I'm almost getting ready to trust nice feelings. But then it all goes very bad.

"Hey! Hey, Quinn! Yo! G. Quinn!"

Gretchen and I both turn. Across the hall, John Montebello and his jock posse are passing, pushing through the crush like a herd of muscle-bound primates. Montebello, looking enormously entertained, is leering at us.

Correction. At me.

"Careful, it might be contagious!"

John Montebello twists his face and puffs out his right

cheek. He begins to walk like a zombie as if his head weighs too much for his body to carry. His buddies, as usual, find him hysterical.

Har-har! Har-de-har-har!

The port-wine hemangioma on my face flares so hot my eyes seem to melt. The hallway is suddenly a blur and my ears are filled with laughter and noises that sound like static. "Leave him alone," a voice somewhere says. I turn and walk. There are people coming at me as if through a fish-eye lens. I have to push around their wide, distorted bodies and between their bulging faces. I have to force myself not to run. When someone grabs at my shoulder, I spin, raising a fist, ready to swing.

Gretchen flinches and backs away a step. The lens snaps back to normal. I can hear again. I drop my hands.

"Are you okay?" Gretchen asks. She's breathing hard. She sounds concerned. It might have been her voice I heard.

"Fine," I say. "Why?" My voice is under control. I'm glad it is. "I gotta get to class, is all."

"We are going to do something, right?"

"Yeah. Sure. We'll figure it out."

"Okay." Gretchen seems to be waiting for me to say something else but I don't.

"Well . . ." she finally says, "okay, see you."

"Yeah," I say. "Great."

Gretchen turns and walks toward her classroom. It occurs to me she might look back and so I spin away and move down the hall. I go to the boy's lavatory on the other side of the school. I go into a toilet stall and lock the door behind me. I don't come out until sometime after lunch.

I solidify my plans.

24

Ephraim's bedroom is a filthy mess of comic books, discarded clothes, DVDs, video game posters, potato chip bags, soda cans, and on a table against the wall, computers in various stages of disrepair. The smell of sweat, mold, unwashed sheets, and pimple cream is even worse.

On Ephraim's Dumpster of a worktable is a Cyber-Power PC Black Pearl computer which comes with two graphic cards; a six core, 12thread chip processor; six gigabytes of RAM; and an 80GB memory board. All told, it costs over four thousand bucks and is the only clean-looking thing in the room.

I've given Ephraim a copy of the local newspaper and explained to him what I want him to do. Thrilled to be of use, Ephraim gets right to work.

Fact.

The first invented computer was called an automatic sequence calculator. It was fifty feet long. It weighed five tons. In 1969, UCLA and Stanford linked computers, creating the first information highway. Almost immediately the first hackers appeared at MIT.

Ephraim is what's known as a green hat. This means he sits in the middle of the modern hacking community somewhere between the black hats who are cybercriminals searching for flaws, glitches, and zero-day vulnerabilities in software and computer networks, and the white hats who are the so-called security experts trying to stop them. It's yet to be determined which direction Ephraim will go. Either way he's going to make a lot of money. United States of Nerd, on the planet Geek.

Sidebar.

Computer engineers and futurists now predict that the event known as the singularity will happen around the year 2036. This is the moment when the intelligence of a single computer will surpass the collective knowledge of all of mankind. It is seen as an *event horizon*, which means no one has any real idea what will happen *after*. It could be Terminator Time. Rise of the Machines. Or it could be the dawning of a brand-new age. As the computers continue to get smarter and smarter, in order to be compatible with them, mankind will choose to merge with them. We'll insert little pea-sized computers into our brains and microscopic machines into our bloodstream to repair our bodies and fight disease. Deus ex machina. God from a machine. We will know everything. We will feel nothing.

Just another thing to look forward to.

The Singularity, of course, is contingent on whether or not the computers don't wake up, take a pixilated look around, and quickly self-destruct in mass horror.

I'm sitting on the edge of the bed, staring at a movie poster of the naked Queen of Sparta telling me *I will not enjoy this*, when Ephraim slams the table in excitement. "Backdoor! I'm in!" he says. He spits the air in disgust. "Puh! Their security isn't even security." He's all smiles. It's taken him all of about a minute and a half. "So what'll it be? Names, addresses, account status? You want it, we got it."

Thirty minutes later sirens are screaming as a fire engine descends on a home one hundred yards up the street from the Landgraf house. Police cars and home security vehicles already line the curb. An hysterical Mexican maid is trying to explain herself to a crowd of distrustful cops.

"*No ladrones! No es un fuego!* No fire! *La alarma no funciona!* Crazy—*loca!*"

Ephraim and I are sitting on the stone wall in front of his driveway watching. Call it a trial run. To prove he can do it, Ephraim has hacked into his neighbor's home security company's database. From there he's burrowed his way into the neighbor's security system where he's activated every alarm in the house. Even I have to admit the results have been both educational and entertaining.

"Told you," says Ephraim, proud of himself.

I'm equally proud of him and have no reason to hide it. I hold out my hand, palm up and open.

"This is between you and me," I say.

Looking excited beyond words, Ephraim taps my open palm with his fist.

"Totally."

25

"I'm goeing 2."

It's written in bold letters on the page of an open spiral notebook.

It's mid-week, late morning, third period English, and Twom, Ephraim, and I are sitting at desks in the back of the classroom. In the front of the room the teacher, Mrs. Soriano, she of the Brillo-pad hair and the hips like a yardstick, is lecturing on the subject of *Beowulf*.

Point of reference.

Beowulf is an epic poem that was written on something other than paper sometime around the eighth century. It is considered one of the most important works of Anglo-Saxon literature and is, needless to say, even more brain paralyzing and irrelevant than Hammurabi.

"Grendel isn't just the enemy, he's a personification of *evil*," Mrs. Soriano says. "He's a *fiend* out of hell, *lusting* for *flesh*, working *evil* in the world." Mrs. Soriano isn't so much talking to the class as she is breathlessly talking to herself. Her eyes are glassy and she keeps licking her lips.

It's like she'd like to have sex with Grendel. Or maybe Beowulf. Or maybe a threesome with both.

I turn to a fresh, clean, lined page in the spiral notebook, scribble a message and show it to Ephraim.

"You suck, Ephraim." I underline "suck." I am truly pissed. Ephraim looks away, guilty. He should be.

"*Beowulf* can be seen as a *naked* battle for not just the *flesh* but the *soul* of the world." In the large, color illustration on the whiteboard, Grendel appears to have a huge penis and a port-wine hemangioma on his face.

"I thoud we wer bruthers, Billy," Twom writes in the notebook.

"We are," I write back.

"R we?" writes Twom. "R we reely? Cuse when yu keep me in the dark, yu miht as well b lying to me. An bros do not ly."

It suddenly seems obvious that text messaging was invented by people with learning disabilities.

"In *Beowulf,* good is not just the opposite of evil," says Mrs. Soriano. "Good is the *avenger* of evil done to us in the past."

"I em in," writes Twom.

"No way," I write.

"If he goes, I do too," writes Ephraim. The brain-dead idiot has opened his own notebook. Unlike Twom's handwriting, which is heavy and clear, Ephraim's scrawl is just about illegible.

"No," I write. "This is my gig." I underline "my."

"<u>ARS</u>," writes Twom. He capitalizes and underlines "ars."

"<u>*EAT ME*</u>." I capitalize, underline, and italicize "eat me."

Twom and Ephraim share a look. Twom nods to Ephraim as if to say, Go ahead.

". . . you need my help to do this," writes Ephraim. He hesitates and then writes the rest of it out fast, as if afraid not to. "Unless we can come . . . I won't." He looks to Twom for approval. Twom nods again. I am truly disgusted. This is so obviously a setup.

"Then *don't!*"

I immediately realize I've sort of blurted this out loud by mistake. It's an appalling loss of control.

"Excuse me! Is there a problem back there?" says Mrs. Soriano. The aggrieved look on her face says that Grendel and Beowulf have pulled out and fled the bed. She's obviously not happy about it.

"No," I say. "We're just comparing notes."

"*Unferth!*" hisses Mrs. Soriano. "Unferth is the Danish warrior who is *unwilling* to *engage evil*, thus proving himself *inferior* to Beowulf!"

When I look back down at my desk. Twom's—or is it Beowulf's?—notebook is back in front of me.

"We R yr whole in th wall gang."

I don't know whether to laugh, scream, or cry. Probably Unferth didn't either. Twom just beams at me, happy as a clam in six feet of water.

I pick up my pen. "<u>Assholes</u> in the wall gang," I write. I close the notebook.

Really, if there was good in the world, it would avenge the evil of people never shutting up, in person or in print.

26

"Count me in," says Deliza.

It's several days later between classes, and through some mysterious but undoubtedly fevered alchemy, Twom and Deliza are an unembarrassed couple now, cruising the halls together, joined at the hip. Grief-stricken, the fat girl, Ophelia, has taken to a nunnery.

"Forget it!" I say. "The whole thing's off."

I can't stand it. Right at the moment, I can't stand them. I turn and start walking. Of course, they follow me.

"Come on, dude," says Twom, "what's one more?"

I shouldn't respond but I do. I should keep on going right to class but I don't. I turn and face them.

"How about five more?" I say. "How about a hundred more? We'll have a party! Invite a cast of thousands! Invite the whole world." Even though I'm practically spitting in his face, Twom doesn't seem remotely perturbed or impressed. I suppose this is to be expected from someone who's used to being arrested.

"Tell me she can keep her mouth shut," I say, gesturing at Deliza. "Tell me. No. Don't bother." I turn to Deliza. "Because you can't!"

Deliza is wearing a sleeveless white top with thin, little lacy straps over her shoulders. She's wearing frayed, cut-off shorts that barely cover the bottom of her butt. Twom has told me Deliza never wears underwear. Along with the shorts, it's an unfair advantage.

"I don't go," she says, "I tell everybody what you're do-ing. And if you don't go, I tell everybody you *planned to*." She smiles pleasantly as if what she's just said remotely makes sense.

"She will, dude," Twom says, loving every minute of it. He begins to chant like a dimwit at a basketball game. "Bill-lee, Bill-lee, Bill-lee, Bill-lee—"

Deliza joins in. Her voice is low and seductive. "Oh, take me, Billy. Ooh, Billy, take me, big boy." She reaches under my chin and gently rubs her fingers up and down my throat, as if she's jerking off my trachea. People are look-ing. People will look at anything. State of the Union ad-dresses. Nervous breakdowns. Guys ejaculating through the top of their heads.

Fact.

Peer pressure is when friends attempt to influence how you think or act. When dealing with peer pressure it is im-portant to analyze the situation, consider the consequences, make a rational decision, and then voice that decision.

"NO WAY!"

Sidebar.

The problem is you have to follow through.

27

It's eleven-thirty at night when we come over the wall into the Aavetzes' backyard.

All is going according to plan.

It has taken Ephraim about two seconds to confirm that newspapers keep their subscribers on an automated database. Unlike the Taylors, most people who go out of town put a hold on their paper over the phone or the Net. The hold is kept on record. Stop date. Start date.

The Aavetz family's last name begins with *A*. Their house is on the flats of High School Highville, not far from the ocean. It is an older neighborhood of medium to large houses. I've walked by and around the Aavetz house three times in the last five days. The front of the house is hidden by a hedge. The metal gate to their front walk is set into two stone pillars. There is a flowered trellis over the gate. The Aavetz family keeps the gate locked. The plaque by the mailbox says they call their house Casa Mañana, which, I hope, translates as "we will be home tomorrow." There is a small sign stuck in the ground. NATIONAL HOME SECURITY.

Ephraim cross-references the Aavetzes' name and address with their security company. National Home Security's data has no record of them being out of town for the weekend but it does have the code to turn off the system. The Aavetz family pays National Home Security forty dollars a month for their due diligence.

The rear of the house is easily accessible from the alley that abuts the Aavetz garage. It's a quick step up onto a rubbish bin and then we climb over the wall. We are not dressed in black. Ephraim wanted to but was told that only morons who have played too many video games wander around in black ninja pants and hoodies late at night. If anyone sees us, we are high school students walking home from the 7-Eleven where the honest shopkeepers have refused to sell us beer. As we hurry up to the back door of the house, I can't help but feel, with some satisfaction, that I've thought of everything.

"The door's locked," Twom says.

I'm totally stunned to realize I haven't thought of everything.

"What do you mean, locked?" says Ephraim.

"Locked is locked, you know what 'locked' means?" says Twom, sounding annoyed.

"What, did you all think it *wouldn't* be?" says Deliza, as if she's talking to a trio of idiot monkeys. "Or did you not think about it at all?" Her aggrieved sigh tells you that the older guys she dates don't make amateur mistakes like this.

I turn the doorknob right, left, right, as if it might have a secret combination that I'm going to stumble on.

"Smart, Billy," says Deliza. "Really smart." Meaning dumb. And I am. All my planning, undone by a doorknob.

"Let's just get out of here before somebody sees us," says Ephraim. His voice is shrill. He's starting to panic. Ephraim's the kind of guy who would panic if a mosquito attacked.

"No," I say. "Just let me think."

"You do that, Billy," says Twom. "You think." Twom steps into the flower bed, picks up a medium-sized rock and tosses it underhand through one of the back door's windowpanes.

"Are you crazy?" says Ephraim, a microsecond before I'm about to say the same thing "You can't break things!"

"Will you shut up?" says Twom. He reaches through and unlocks the door from the inside. The alarm goes off as he opens the door and enters. We all scramble through after him, circus clowns clambering out of a miniature car. The alarm is wailing. I turn to Ephraim. Our tech man. Our expert. Unflappable.

"What's the security code, Ephraim?"

"We've got to get out of here!" says Ephraim.

"Shut up, you asshole," says Deliza.

"Ephraim, the code!" I say.

"*You* shut up!" says Ephraim, glaring at Deliza.

"Don't tell her to shut up!" says Twom, pushing Ephraim.

"The code, Ephraim!"

"I'm leaving," says Ephraim. He looks like he might cry.

"Ephraim," I say, raising my voice, "what's the code!"

"I don't know what I *did* with it!"

"Aw, shit," mutters Twom. He looks resigned, as if yet again a punishable crime he's involved himself in isn't going quite according to plan.

I grab Ephraim by the shirt collar. His face is pasty white with fear. His pimples stand out like polka dots. His breath would kill an elephant.

"Ephraim," I say. "The code." I'm very quiet. "Please. "

Trembling, Ephraim reaches into his pants pocket. He comes out with a small, wadded slip of paper. It looks like a spitball, something you'd blow out a straw.

"Good," I say, letting him go. "Take your time. No mistakes."

Ephraim nods. He unwraps the spitball. Glancing at the paper, Ephraim punches in the security code, carefully hitting the keys one at a time. The alarm stops. We breathe a collective sigh of relief. We collectively jump out of our skins as the telephone rings. I let it ring twice more. I answer.

"Hello," I say.

"This is National Home Security," says the voice on the phone. "We have a signal here that your alarm has gone off?"

For their forty dollars a month, I'm sure the Aavetz family will be happy to know that National Home Security is on the job.

"Yeah, sorry," I say. "We were coming home, my Dad accidentally broke a window."

"May I have your password, please," says National Home Security.

"Just a second," I say. I cover the phone's mouthpiece with a hand. "Password?" I say to Ephraim.

Ephraim looks at the little slip of paper. He squints.

"Tickety-boo," says Ephraim.

"What the fuck kind of a password," says Twom, "is—"

Deliza shushes him, cutting him off. "You're sure?" I say to Ephraim. "It's not Tickety-Bill or Tickety-Bob, it's Tickety-boo?"

Ephraim nods. "Tickety-boo," he says.

"Tickety-boo," I say to the phone.

"Thank you and have a nice night," says the voice of the National Security Company. They hang up. Ephraim, Twom, and Deliza are staring at me with nervous, expectant faces. I let them sweat for a moment.

"We're in," I say.

28

We're like forest children who have never been inside a house before. Once we know we're safe, we make ourselves at home.

Ephraim hits the kitchen. In the cupboard he finds Fritos and cookies. In the refrigerator, he finds ice cream and cans of soda. He takes his stash into the family room where he finds an old Sony PlayStation and some first- and second-generation video games. He is like a collector who has stumbled upon a horde of valuable antiques, and he settles in, thrilled and happy, noshing and nuking.

Twom and Deliza are already pulling off their clothes as they go running down the hall. Their plan is simple. The house is one big honeymoon suite and they are going to christen every room.

I explore. The Aavetz house is low-key in a way that reminds me of Gretchen's. The furniture is old, used-looking stuff but polished and well maintained. There are sterling silver bowls and trays on sideboards which, if I was a thief, would be out the door already. Mr. Aavetz is an audiophile who listens to jazz and classical music on vinyl records using a Clearaudio Concept turntable. Mrs. Aavetz seems to like crossword puzzles. Judging by the photographs they have a son and a daughter, both married. They have two grandchildren. Mr. Aavetz drives a Toyota hybrid, Mrs. Aavetz an old Audi station wagon.

The Aavetzes sleep in separate bedrooms. Mr. Aavetz's bed is covered by a plaid cotton quilt. There are books and reading glasses next to the bed. Mr. Aavetz likes biographies. Mrs. Aavetz's bed is the bed they used to share. It's a king. It's covered by a white cotton duvet. Mrs. Aavetz likes to read crime thrillers and mysteries.

I sit on Mrs. Aavetz's bed. It has a pleasant smell to it, like something freshly washed. The cotton of the duvet has a high thread count and is very smooth. I settle back. The ceiling is plastered. The way it's been applied, in broad swirls, makes you think of clouds. I can sleep here. There are no dreams or ghosts in the Aavetzes' house, or if there are, they're not mine.

I close my eyes.

When I look up, the digital clock on the bedside table reads 1:13 A.M. I've only been asleep for about an hour and a half but I feel rested. The house is quiet. There is the smell of bacon in the air.

The others are in the kitchen.

Everything in the fridge and most of what was in cupboards and drawers is now on the counter. Deliza is cooking. Twom and Ephraim are at a table. Twom is drinking red wine from a bottle while Ephraim eats yet more ice cream. They are engaged in heated conversation.

"He's a psycho," says Ephraim.

"He's the Dark Knight!" says Twom.

"What are they talking about?" I say to Deliza.

Deliza goes "tsk" which, unlike "mmm," is a way of implying something negative like annoyance, impatience, or disgust. "*Comic* books," she says. She shakes her head as if to say she can't believe males are even remotely related to human beings.

"Superman would destroy Batman!" says Ephraim.

"In what?" says Twom. "That blue and red leotard? What's he gonna do, blow Batman to death? Maybe squeeze his dick off when he takes it up the ass?"

Twom is clearly enjoying himself. Ephraim, who each summer spends every waking minute at Comic-Con dressed as a Jedi knight, is on the verge of going drool-sputtering ballistic.

"Superman is invulnerable! He can fly, he has heat vision, he can do anything!"

"He's a pussy," says Twom.

"I didn't know you cooked," I say to Deliza.

It's not just bacon. She's made scrambled eggs with cheese, sautéed onion, and mushrooms. She's wearing an apron she's found and her dark hair is pulled back in a ponytail. Her makeup has wiped off during her sack diving with Twom and she's suddenly pretty as opposed to outright sexy.

"I cook if I feel like it," Deliza says. "I just don't clean." She hands me a plate and silverware.

Plate in hand, I turn from the stove, walk over to the table and sit just in time to hear Ephraim seal the deal.

"Superman really exists," he says.

Twom almost spits wine on the table.

"You are so full of it, dude."

"In 1931," says Ephraim, "a spaceship crashed in Idaho. A trapper saw it go down. When he got there, he found a little boy."

Deliza puts plates down on the table and sits. We all begin eating.

"He took the boy to his cabin," says Ephraim. "He tried to talk to him but the boy didn't speak any language the trapper had ever heard of."

"He's a trapper," says Twom. "What languages *would* he have heard of?"

"Shshh," says Deliza. She puts her hand on Twom's. "What happened to him?" She's not teasing, she's curious now.

"Soldiers arrived. The boy tried to fight. He was strong beyond belief. But there were too many of them. He was taken away. The crash site was cleared. No one would know it was ever there. One year later, Jerome Siegel and Joe Schuster came out with the first Superman comic. It was commissioned by the government, part of a plot to throw people off. It almost succeeded."

Ephraim's voice is quiet and very serious. It's easy to

believe this story of a child, caged and studied by adults who don't know what else to do with him.

"He's aged slowly. He's a young man now. They keep him behind steel walls. They know how strong he is. They know he's angry. They know one day he's gonna break out. And that's the day he'll have his revenge. On *everyone*."

Ephraim eats a hugely satisfied spoonful of ice cream. His eggs sit, untouched. "Superman," he says, "is not a pussy."

29

When Mom and Gretchen see one another, they both call out each other's name, rush forward, fall into each other's arms and begin to cry.

"Oh, Gretchen!" cries Mom.

"Oh, Mrs. Kinsey!" says Gretchen.

It's a Saturday afternoon, Dad has taken his bicycles to the desert to practice getting injured, and at Mom's suggestion, I've invited Gretchen over so she can say hi.

"You're all grown-up," says Mom.

"I've missed you so much," says Gretchen.

"You're so *beautiful*," says Mom.

But now, somewhere in the middle of all the female gushing and cooing, Mom's happy tears turn into something else. She tries to smile as she strokes Gretchen's hair. She sort of hums in her throat as she stares into Gretchen's eyes. And then she puts her hand over her mouth and she begins to cry. *Really* cry. She clutches Gretchen and lets it all go, not loud but choking, deep and guttural. Somehow Gretchen seems to know exactly what to do. She holds

Mom. She caresses her cheek. It's like she's the parent and Mom's the child.

"It's all right," Gretchen says. "I know," she says. "I know."

It takes a lot of deep breaths and starts and restarts but Mom finally pulls it back together and they beam at one another. Mom looks totally spent, like she's had some kind of monster emotional orgasm and Gretchen looks like she's been happy and honored to help.

"Come in the kitchen and tell me all about you," says Mom.

"I want to," says Gretchen.

Nobody asks me to, but I tag along.

"So are you two a couple?" Mom and Gretchen have been going for what seems like an hour now—there have been tuna sandwiches, there has been iced tea—and Mom says this like she suspects or hopes we are. And I guess after you've sobbed your guts out and shared tuna and tea with people, you feel like there should be no secrets, but still, it's embarrassing as all get out.

"We're just friends," I say, uncomfortable.

"We're just catching up," says Gretchen, semimortified.

"Being friends is a good place to start," says Mom, acting all wise and mysterious on us. You can tell that in her mind she's already picking out bed linens and silver patterns for us, and all of a sudden Gretchen and I can't get out of the kitchen fast enough.

We go outside. It's one of those brilliant late fall

afternoons that only a Mediterranean climate, global warming, and ever-rising ocean levels can create. It is mid-seventies and sunny and the sky is an impossible blinding blue.

"I'm really glad you're here," I tell Gretchen. And I am. Since the incident in the school hallway, PDAs—public displays of affection or, in my case, public displays of *attention*—have been seriously avoided. I haven't known *what* to do. It's great to see her.

We've decided to take a swim. Gretchen has gone into the poolhouse and when she comes out she's wearing a bright yellow string bikini. She's slim, with small, high breasts. Her pale skin is dusted with freckles. Her ass is perfect.

This is how it works.

Visual stimuli produce neurotransmitters that race through the body's parasympathetic nervous system. Nitric oxide triggers arterial dilatation. Blood rushes into expanding spongy cells, where it's trapped and held by the subtunical venular plexuses.

Translation? I have wood.

I stand there frozen, not sure if I'm supposed to be proud or mortified that my dick is pushing at the waistband of my board shorts. If Gretchen notices, she doesn't let on. Turning away, she puts her towel down on a lounge chair. She reaches for suntan lotion. The thought of her rubbing it on makes it a good moment to dive into the water, and unnerved, I land in a graceless, jarring belly flop.

"How's the water?" Gretchen says. The water is freezing. My wood has reversed direction and, along with my nuts, taken refuge somewhere deep in my stomach cavity.

"Great," I say. "Come on in."

The entire afternoon becomes imbued with an intense aura of sex. I feel as if there's a giant magnifying glass overhead, turning the sun's rays into a focused laser beam that's aimed directly at my gonads. Anything even vaguely oblong—a water bottle, a cement pestle on the adjacent wall, a small cactus in the garden—reminds me of an erect penis. Anything furrowed or with a hole—a pool ring, a flower, the sight of glistening water cradled in Gretchen's belly button, even the crease I see when I hold my thumb and forefinger together—makes me think of Gretchen's shielded crotch. Time and time again, I drop into the freezing pool. I tread water until my balls ache. It's finally all too much, and excusing myself, I go running into the poolhouse where, with hardly half a dozen strokes, I whack off into the sink. The first ejaculation actually hits the mirror and when I look at it, I see with some fascination that the hemangioma on my cheek and the knob of my dick are the exact same flushed, purple color.

There's not enough Kleenex in the world.

Coming back out and across the deck, I suddenly worry Gretchen will smell the Clorox fragrance of cum on my hand and so once again, without thinking, I jump into the icy pool.

"Who wants homemade lemonade?" Mom calls from the upper terrace. The afternoon now is officially Ozzie and Harriet with a freezing, half-flaccid, Grendel hard-on.

Historical footnote.

The Adventures of Ozzie and Harriet was the longest-running sitcom in U.S. television history until it was overtaken by *The Simpsons* in 2004. Unlike *The Simpsons*, which is about a normal, dysfunctional, modern-day family, it presented an idealized family in the 1950s where fathers solved problems, mothers were nurturing, and children were high achievers. The show can be accessed on the online video service Hulu, under "parody."

Later, against all protocol, but desperate for something that might budge my brains from my scrotum back up into my cranium, I take Gretchen down to the drum room. And as I lead her through the door, for the first time ever, I realize it is an airless compartment that reeks of mildew, sweat, and lug oil. No one but me has been in here for at least a year.

"Wow," Gretchen murmurs. I can't tell if she's impressed or appalled by all the gear. "You must be good."

"Not really," I say.

"I don't believe you," she says. She gives me a look that says she knows I'm being all modest because I'm really hot stuff. And even if I wasn't, I feel like I am now.

"Give it a try," I say. She sits. She picks up two sticks. Giggling, she wraps a cymbal. She whomps the bass drum a few times and does a slow ragged roll on the snare. She giggles again. She begins to bang the shit out of everything at once. She squints her eyes, opens her mouth wide, and shakes her head around, her hair flying, as if she's some wild-ass rock drummer. It's pretty amusing actually.

"Now you," she says, and before I can remember my vow never to play in front of people, I'm sitting down. I pick up some tympani mallets. I want a more muted sound. I do a fast, soft roll across the rack toms, high to low, then continue down to the floor toms. I reverse it, low to high, finishing with a quick riff on each cymbal bell.

"That was *unbelievable!*" says Gretchen.

I am now serious putty to be molded by her hands.

I begin to move around the set, changing the patterns, using the bass drums for accents and fills. I stop. I start again. Cannibal sounds. Human flesh as food. Blood as ambrosia. And as I begin to change the tempo, I realize it's all come back to sex again, that the beat of the bass drum is the body, that the crash of the cymbal is the breath, and that the rhythmic patterns that make up the world around are all about desire.

It's a beautiful day.

30

Perhaps it's Ephraim's story of Superman but Twom starts having flying dreams.

Flying dreams fall under the category of lucid dreams, which means you are aware that you're dreaming. To fly in a dream symbolizes the desire to break free of restrictions and limitations.

In Twom's dreams, the sun is shining and the sky is vast and blue. He can see waves breaking and the ground moving swiftly by down below. He can see the tops of houses and cars creeping along like bugs.

He feels ecstasy.

Twom tells us that one night he's joined in his dreams by me, Deliza, and then Ephraim. We fly together as if in formation, Twom leading us, all of us soaring as one. In the dream, Twom says, we finally turn like a flock of birds and fly away. Toward light. Toward Neverland. A place where you never age. You never grow up. Never return from.

My dreams continue to be more grounded. I'm on a road. It is a desolate road. It is a cold, bleak day. There is no sign of life. No animals. No birds. No people. The trees are without leaves. I'm standing at a bus stop. I'm confused. I'm not sure why I'm here. And then across the road, I see her. She's appeared from nowhere. Dorie wears pink pajamas beneath a light blue hospital robe. Her feet are bare. Her eyes are enormous in her hairless head. I wave. Dorie smiles but doesn't move. And then she's lost from view as, all of a sudden, a big silver bus pulls in front of her. When the bus pulls away, Dorie is gone. I stand there. On a empty road. Alone. No idea where I am. No way home.

"Billy?"

Startled, I jerk my eyes open. I'm in a chair in the family room. Mom is in front of me. She picks up the remote and turns off the television. She's wearing an expensive-looking light blue dress. Her hair is up and her makeup is done.

"You should get ready," she says. She looks like she wants to say more but she doesn't. She turns and walks away.

You will never cease to be a presence in our lives. Rather than an ache, your voice will hover like the faintest beating of wings over our heads, to remind us how much we loved you. And do now.

A year after Dorie's death, Mom got the idea that we should celebrate her life. And so every year since then, on Dorie's birthday, that's what we do. We dress up. We go to the cemetery where Dorie's ashes are buried. Mom

invites people and everyone who comes—relatives, neighbors, family friends—brings flowers. Really, you could
sneeze to death.

It's nice that Gretchen's here this year.

Nobody says much of anything. We stare at the headstone. It reads "Dorothy Kinsey" and tells you the year
Dorie was born and the year she died. If you didn't take
the time to do the math there's nothing there to tell you
she was only eleven years old. Some minister Mom has
found says a prayer. Every year it seems like it's a different guy but they always say the same, stupid prayer.

"The Lord is my Shepherd, I shall not want."

I guess it's supposed to be comforting. Pastures and
quiet waters and soul restoration should be. But all it makes
me think of is that Dorie was a little girl who died way
too young.

The world is filled with Dories.

After the prayer, Mom, who's about to lose it any second, puts this special bouquet she's brought onto Dorie's
grave. It's made of white daisies. Innocence.

Then it's Dad's turn. Dad steps forward and puts down
a single orchid. An orchid is the symbol of perfection.
The spots on an orchid represent the blood of Christ.
They're also the color of the wine that Gordon will consume in vast quantities the minute we get back home. To
cut him some slack, he looks like he needs it. He's pale.
His eyes are like stones. Dorie was his favorite. Dorie
was everyone's favorite.

Now it's my turn. I put a calla lily down close to Dorie's

headstone. The blossom—the spathe—is an intense white. The flower stalk—the spadix—is a blazing yellow. Calla lilies represent purity and chastity and are often placed on the graves of young people who have suffered untimely deaths.

We all stand there as if we're trying to feel Dorie on the afternoon breeze.

According to the so-called experts, grief is an emotional response to loss. No two people deal with it alike. Grief devastates marriages and destroys families. Profound grief makes you question life itself.

Maybe. Maybe not.

But the world was a much happier place before Dorie got sick. Dad talked about starting his own construction company. Mom was into Girl Scout troops and the PTA. Dorie and I would laugh together as the two of them close-danced around the kitchen, Dad bellowing Bruce Springsteen at the top of his lungs. All was safe and right with the world. Bad things and sad things happened to other people. Only good things happened to the Kinseys.

After all. We'd won the lottery.

31

There are eighteen lit candles on the cake Mom brings out at dinner that night. Mom and Dad and Gretchen, who's stayed for dinner, sing "Happy Birthday" to me. It's been a pleasant time. It really has. There have been presents. Mom has given me some shirts that I won't wear.

"It's the thought that counts."

Dad has given me a hundred-dollar bill plus a bottle of wine that I'll never drink.

"Eighteen, birthday boy! That's legal somewhere!"

Gretchen has given me a CD she's burned of what she says is all her favorite music.

"You don't have to like it."

"I know I will," I say. And I mean it.

But now as they all sing, the day catches up with Mom and her eyes fill. And no Springsteen anymore; Dad's idea of singing is to mumble. Even Gretchen, sensing something's off, grows quiet. I pretend to make a wish and then, smiling, blow all the candles out. "Wow, this looks awesome!" I say.

Point of reference.

The early Greeks believed that the smoke of their birthday candles carried their wishes to the gods in heaven.

The smoke from my candles rises like gray ribbons to the ceiling where it stops and gathers and, unable to ascend further, sits there like a small, dark nimbus cloud.

"Who wants cake?"

32

I find there are over one million search results for picking locks on the Internet.

Why am I not surprised?

There are Web sites. There are videos. There are guidebooks. There are forums and chat rooms for amateurs, students, and professionals alike. Online stores sell you everything you need, as if picking the locks to safes, doors, cars, and houses is a quaint little hobby for the terminally bored.

From Picklock Parts & Supplies, LLC, I order a SouthOrd Twenty Piece Lock Pick Set with reinforced stainless steel handles. According to the site, the MPXS20 contains fourteen rustproof, nickel-plated steel picks, a broken-key extractor, and five tension tools. Also included is a luggage-quality zippered case, a dead bolt lock and cylinder with a cutaway section, and a CD entitled *The Visual Guide to Lock Picking*, which, they proclaim, "will have you picking locks like a pro in no time!" At $48.95, this seems like a bargain.

I pay by cash through Ulti-Pay, an online company that assures me they understand that paying by credit card is *"not the right answer for every merchant and every consumer."* The italics are theirs.

To hide a birthmark, you need an opaque concealer that has a higher level of pigment and a heavier consistency than average makeup. The one on the bottom shelf of the local CVS is called Killer Cover Total Blockout. The label tells me that this revolutionary waterproof, smudgeproof, perspiration- and heat-resistant formula covers the most difficult flaws that traditional concealers can't touch and that its highly pigmented formula stays put until removed. Killer Cover includes five colors to be used alone or blended to achieve a perfect match and can be used to cover up depigmentations, spider veins, bruises, tattoos, and yes, port-wine hemangiomas.

Wow.

It's like putting Silly Putty on your skin, thick, sticky, and heavy. When I'm done, the face that stares back at me out of the mirror is almost unrecognizable to me. Ephraim would be jealous. It's like I have a new secret identity.

Normal Man.

I get on the bus and go downtown. I go into a nondescript store called Mailboxes and More. Mailboxes and More is an establishment that prints, copies, ships, binds, sells packing materials and holiday cards, and yes, rents mailboxes. The clerk, a stoned-looking college kid, tells me I need an ID to rent a mailbox. I tell him I left it at home. He shrugs and tells me to bring it next time. Using cash, I rent the mailbox under the name of John Montebello.

I admit to myself I'm having a good time.

I wait ten days.

Donning my mask of Killer Cover Total Blockout, I go downtown to Mailboxes and More again. I go in and open my rented mailbox. It is stuffed with junk mail. In the middle of the junk mail is an easy-to-miss delivery slip. I toss the junk mail and give the slip to the same bored clerk. The clerk takes it, goes into the back, and after what seems like half an hour, comes out and hands me a box shipped UPS ground service. He asks to see an ID. Darn, I tell him, I left it at home again. He shrugs and tells me to bring it next time. I sign for it. John Montebello.

"You should do something about the junk mail," I say.

"Like what?" he says.

The voice on *The Visual Guide to Lock Picking* starts off by telling me that you never know where and when you may need to pick a lock. You might be locked out of your house or car or—*"you may be captured by insurgents in a foreign country."*

Just another thing to look forward to.

The illustrations are large, simple, and in color.

The Visual Guide tells and shows that the locks on most dead bolts, doorknobs, and cars are pin tumbler locks. These are locks that are made up of a cylinder, inside of which is a rotating plug. Drilled into the cylinder shaft and plug are four or five holes. In the holes, two pins fit on top of each other. The pin on top is spring-loaded, and called the driving pin. The pin below is the key pin. The teeth of a key, says the voice, when put into the cylinder, pushes all the key pins into their individual, proper alignment. When the pins are aligned, the plug is free to rotate and the lock will open.

After reversing and replaying the close-up illustrated sequence of the key driving into the cylinder—a sequence that seems decidedly sexual but then, at the age of eighteen, most things do—I decide that this is an overly complicated way of saying I should use the tension wrench to put pressure on the plug while I use the picks to pop the pins into alignment, one by one.

It sounds easy. A monkey could do it.

I can't.

I put too much tension on the tension wrench. I put too little. Using the pick, I pop a key pin out. When I move the pick, the driving pin pops the key pin back. I'm almost to the third pin when the pick slips and I put a good half inch of it into my left index finger.

I return the SouthOrd Twenty Piece Lock Pick Set minus cylinder and video via FedEx. I go back online and order the all stainless steel SouthOrd EZ Snap Lock Pick Gun, which, Picklock Parts & Supplies, LLC, tells me, allows you to open locks with minimal instruction. The EZ pick, Picklock Parts & Supplies, LLC, informs me, is "a great tool for law enforcement, first responders, property managers, storage unit owners," and *those who need to open pin tumbler locks in quick succession."* At $49.99, it, too, sounds like a bargain.

I pay by cash through Ulti-Pay. I wait five days, put on my mask and, as Normal Man, go down to Mailboxes and More. I collect my EZ pick. The clerk and I are on a first-name basis. "Ey, dude"—"Sapp'nin', bro." The ID is never mentioned.

Unlike the lock picks, which have a certain sense of practical beauty to them, the EZ pick has the aesthetics of a skinny-nosed squirt gun. Taking my practice lock, I use a tension wrench to put a slight pressure on the cylinder, insert the EZ pick, and pull the trigger twice. It makes a grating sound. The plug rotates. The lock opens.

Technology!

33

Bad locks, like good fences, make great neighbors.

We establish a routine. Ephraim, who proves to be not just gifted at breaking and entering but truly excited by it, goes online and hacks into the local newspaper's database. He finds a house that has put its paper delivery on hold. Taking the name from the database, he hacks into airline Web sites and does a preprogrammed search through their passenger lists to see if the name comes up. If and when it does, Twom and I do a quick surveillance to make sure the exterior of the house is up to our standards and that no house sitter is staying there while the owners are gone. We get the name of the owner's security company off the sign they always seem to put in the flower bed. Ephraim hacks into the security company's database and comes out with security codes and passwords.

We take Deliza's Mercedes. The car is her mother's but she pretty much has full-time access to it, and it says something about the neighborhoods we operate in that it doesn't stand out on the street. Anything less, a clunker or pickup or an old van, for instance, would. We decide that if anyone should ever ask, we're looking for the Montebello house. We heard there was a party. But they don't. Late at night there are hardly even any cars passing on the street.

We keep to the shadows at first but soon realize it's not necessary. We realize that people who live behind walls and gates don't want to know what's going on outside. They have no need for or interest in one another. No one, unless it's the maid, is going next door to borrow a cup of sugar.

We go over the wall. Or up the walk. Or around to the back. I use the EZ pick to open the front door. Or the side door. Or the back door. Ephraim turns off the security alarm. If the security firm calls, we give them the password.

Each house is different.

Different floors, different layouts, different furniture. Different dishware. Big rooms. Small rooms. Different artwork on different-colored walls. Children's scribbles. Museum pieces. Different foods in the refrigerator. Different liquor in the cupboard.

In each house, we all do pretty much the same thing. If there's a computer, Ephraim is on it, eating anything unhealthy and playing several online games at once. If there's no computer, he watches television. As there are seven hundred and forty televisions per thousand people in the United States and as the average American watches over thirty hours of television a week, five to six hours a day, most of them with the sound on, there's always a television. Often in every room.

In each house, Twom and Deliza go to town. On beds, on floors, on couches, in chairs, in baths and showers with the water running. They are tireless. Their gasps and groans and mewings fill the air. In one home, I enter a room and find them lying naked and inverted on a Persian rug. Twom's face is between Deliza's legs. Her dark hair spills over his thighs. They are oblivious to everything but themselves, and embarrassed and feeling as if I'm intruding on something that's not my business, I quickly retreat.

As for me, I find that I am fascinated by the people who live in these houses. In knowing about them. In discovering what they only reveal to one another. I look at their books to see what they read. I go through their mail. I am more than a mere thief, I am a voyeur into their lives. I go through their drawers and closets to study what clothes they wear. I am captivated by their photos. They smile. They stick out their tongues and make funny faces. They gape in surprise, hair tousled, as they're getting out of bed. They wear wedding gowns and morning suits. They giggle by picnic tables, float ducks in bathtubs. They are on water skis and camping trips. They stand in front of Broadway marquees and pose in front of the pyramids. They stick their heads through Coney Island cutouts that make them look like musclemen and bathing beauties. They hold newborn babies that become toddlers that become teenagers. They hug filmy-eyed geriatrics.

I realize I am looking at the best parts of their lives. I am looking at the highlights. These are the respite moments that have made them happy. These are the jewels on a bridge of sighs. Other than prescription drugs and dirty dishes, there are usually few clues as to what might make any of them despair. Perhaps that's why I can finally do what I have come to do. I lie back on one of their beds. I close my eyes. I gratefully and dreamlessly sleep.

At the end of the night we all end up in the same place. It is Ephraim who begins this ritual, settling back in the living room, searching for the horror movies he likes on television. Twom and Deliza come into the room, hesitate a moment, then join him on the couch. Light flickers off their rapt faces. I watch from the door. They could be a family of cavemen or a pack of wolves, staring intently into the fire as the screams on the wind grow loud then fade to deathly silence, only to rise and shriek again. They huddle close, more for safety than warmth.

The golden age of horror movies was the fifties and it's generally accepted that movies then—*Them!*, *It Came from Beneath the Sea*, *Invaders from Mars*, *Creature from the Black Lagoon*—were a reflection of the nation's collective unconscious fears shaped by the threat of the atomic bomb and the fear of total annihilation.

Horror still rules.

Only today it's knives, drills, torture chambers, and

chain saws. It's demons in human form wearing puppet faces and hockey masks. It's the walking dead, rotting from the inside out, hungry for brains.

What are we collectively afraid of now? As I stand in the doorway watching, Dorie whispers the answer in my ear.

"Each other."

34

Fact.

How we prepare and share food says a lot about who we are as people.

For as many nights each week as Mom sets the table and lights the candles in the big dining room and tries to engage Dad and me in meaningful conversation, there are a lot of times when the housekeeper doesn't cook before she leaves, and where other than to say "pass the pizza," we eat in the kitchen in silence, each of us in our own world, semioblivious to one another. Mom picks the pepperoni off her slice. Dad contemplates the "tears" in his wine glass. Sometimes I read a book. I'm not so crazy about pizza but it's delivered and so when Mom doesn't cook, we eat a fair amount of it. So do a ton of people. Over three billion pizzas a year are sold in the United States. It works out to over two hundred million square feet a month. Dad's good for fifty square feet all by himself. It goes well with a Zinfandel.

. . .

Fact.

Eating as a family decreases a teenager's risk of anti-social behavior.

I'm at Twom's grandmother's house. The house is in one of the "poorer" sections of High School Highville, a neighborhood where about fifty years ago all the maids and cooks and maintenance people who worked in the rich houses lived. The small, bungalow-style houses are in walking distance of the beach and now go for close to a million a pop. Twom's grandmother's house is a tear-down if ever I saw one. The lawn is an unwatered, rock-hard piece of dirt so inhospitable the weeds have moved to the flower beds. The outside of the house is an un-maintainable eyesore and the inside suggests that Twom's grandmother is a fan of the TV show *Hoarders,* especially if hoarders hoard overflowing ashtrays. Twom says it wasn't always like this. He says his grandfather, who once upon a time did all the work around the place and kept things totally shipshape, finally gave up and died just to get away from his wife.

For dinner, Twom has announced we're going to order—what else?—*pizza,* and now for no apparent rea-son this has prompted Twom's grandmother to decide that, no, she's going to cook. Twom's reaction suggests that this isn't necessarily a physical act that produces food.

"Just give me some money to order a fucking pizza," Twom says to his grandmother. "Is that too much to ask?"

Twom's grandmother has a large glass of gin in one hand and a lit cigarette in the other and is obviously half in the bag. Her four Jack Russell terriers keep running around the room, all of them barking. One more dog and the house would legally be declared a kennel.

"You don't invite guests over and order some *dago* pizza, not in *my* house," Twom's grandmother says. "I'm making your friend a nice, home-cooked meal."

"You couldn't cook home-cooked shit," says Twom.

Twom's grandmother is one these older women who's still trying to look like a teenager. There are a lot of them in High School Highville. She has peroxided blond hair and the stretched, protruding cheekbones that come with a second or third face-lift. She's wearing neon-blue pants and a sequined top. She has long, fake, painted fingernails which draw immediate attention to her swollen, arthritic knuckles. If the thought wasn't truly, totally terrifying I'd say she wants to cook me dinner as a way of coming on to me. Really, some if not most people should be obligated to die by forty.

"What are you saying?" Twom's grandmother says, squinting through her cloud of cigarette smoke. It's an odd question. Twom was pretty clear. "Are you saying I can't cook?" This, too, is an odd question because if Twom wasn't saying this, he was certainly implying it.

"Will you just fuck off and give me the money for pizza?" says Twom.

"For forty years, I cooked," says Twom's grandmother.

Her eyes are bugging. She's starting to raise her voice. "I taught your mother to cook!"

"She cooks ptomaine poisoning," says Twom. Ptomaine refers to the taste and smell of putrefying animal flesh. If you look the word up on thefreedictionary.com, you'll find that the site is sponsored by McDonald's.

Twom's grandmother starts stomping around the kitchen, slamming drawers and saying things like, "Oh! Of all the ungrateful—selfish-selfish!" Stuff like that. The Jack Russells are starting to go ballistic, yapping and scurrying around, bouncing off walls and attempting to dig through the floor with their claws.

"Give! Me! Money!" says Twom.

Twom's grandmother throws her cigarette in the sink where it sizzles. "No!" she says, stamping her foot like a stubborn little kid. "I'm! Cooking!"

Thirty minutes later Twom and I sit at the kitchen table watching as Twom's grandmother, now completely and colossally blasted, stands at the stove, seemingly puzzled. The kitchen smoke alarm is howling. The pans on the stove, as well as the stovetop, are in flames. The Jack Russell terriers sit in a tight little group, paralyzed with fear. Twom's grandmother suddenly decides it would be a good idea to douse the fire and she throws her drink at the blazing pans. The alcohol ignites. The flames hit the exhaust hood above the stove. The Jack Russells trample one another to death in their haste to scramble out of the kitchen.

"Willard!" Twom's grandmother screams. "Order pizza!"

.   .   .

Fact.

Kids who eat with their parents are forty percent more likely to get As and Bs in school!

Twom and I are over at Ephraim's house. We are in the family room, which seems to be another large, sterile room in another large, empty house where no family ever gathers. A raging brawl is in progress in the kitchen. It's been going on for at least forty minutes and is entering the sixth round.

"Read the recipe!" screams Ephraim's mother. "It says cumin! Do you know what cumin is?"

"Jews do not eat cumin!" screams Ephraim's father.

"It's kosher cumin!" shrieks Ephraim's mother.

Crash. Yell. Shriek.

"Now it's kosher shit!" yells Ephraim's father.

"Five bucks on Dad," says Twom.

Scream. Yell. Crash.

"Do not touch my osso buco, Mira, I'm warning you, do not touch the osso buco!" *Osso buco* is Italian for "bone with a hole." It's a dish people once had to eat in order not to starve to death, and because most gourmets never *had* to eat it, they now consider it a delicacy.

Yell. Crash. Scream.

"You—bitch!"

"Do I hear ten?" says Twom.

Scream. Collide. Thud. Shriek.

It sounds like knives are coming out of drawers.

Ephraim doesn't look so much embarrassed as he does totally depressed and miserable.

"Want to order a pizza?" he moans.

Fact.

Adolescent girls who have frequent family meals are less likely to have eating disorders.

They don't eat pizza at the Baraza house.

Twom has been invited by Deliza to have dinner with her family and he has brought me along, he tells me, for moral support. Moral support means giving support to a person without making any contribution beyond encouragement.

I'm hardly needed.

Deliza and her parents eat dinner in a vaulted room that looks like something out of Versailles. There are white-uniformed maids in attendance. They all have the dark, expressionless faces of Aztec statues. Twom and I are sitting under a chandelier at a twenty-foot table with Deliza's mother. She has a tired look on her heavily made-up face, the look of someone who wishes they were anywhere but here. She keeps looking at the hemangioma on my right cheek as if it might be a parasitic, flesh-eating virus. Deliza and her father are just outside the dining room doors having an argument. In Spanish.

"Is there a reason you've brought this imbecile into our home?"

Or something like that.

"Yes! Because it pisses you off."

Or something like that.

"If you're fucking this freak, I'll kill both of you."

Or something like that.

"I'll fuck him on the dining room table if I want to!"

The Aztec maids, faces dark against their frilly collars and white caps, don't so much as blink.

"Pass the burritos," says Twom. He's having a great time.

"Chicken Kiev," says Deliza's lifeless mother.

Fact.

The average parent spends 38.5 minutes per week in meaningful conversation with their children.

Strangest of all is eating food at Gretchen's house. Gretchen has invited me to Sunday dinner and I'm at the table with the entire family: Jim, Kath, Gretchen, Gretchen's college-age older brother, Bob, and her two younger sisters, Suzie and Sara. It turns out the Quinns are all vegetarians, and after starting the meal with a blessing—"God, who gives to us this food . . ."—we are eating pasta with tomatoes, white beans, and spinach, a grilled vegetable medley, and warm crusty bread. The pasta is topped with crumbled feta and it's awesome. Everyone is talking and laughing at the same time. It's like being to dinner at the Waltons'.

Historical footnote.

The Waltons was a television show about this extended family living in poverty in the mountains of Virginia during the Great Depression. Even though they're poor and uneducated, the family is loving and supportive. The adults are wise, the kids are well-meaning and respect-ful, and at the end of every episode they all individually say good night to one another, calling out from their dif-ferent poverty-stricken bedrooms. The show is occasion-ally on late-night cable but can be accessed on the online video service Hulu, under the genre of science fiction.

Just like the Waltons, Gretchen's family has *conver-sations* at the dining room table. You can disagree but aren't allowed to get angry. You're allowed to tease but not to hurt feelings. You're expected to be respectful and open-minded to other's opinions and engaged, commit-ted, and interested in the conversation. It's the most bi-zarre thing I've ever experienced and I can't help but marvel and pay attention.

"The Marshalls' house was broken into," Dr. Quinn says.

It comes out of nowhere, making my ears totally perk up, which is a stupid figure of speech because ears are made of cartilage and incapable of independent movement.

"No. When?" says Mrs. Quinn

"About a week ago," says Dr. Quinn. "I ran into Jack at the hospital. He said they went in through the back door. Had the alarm code, the password. He and Kim are won-dering if it could be someone at their security company."

"Did they steal stuff?" says Gretchen's sister Suzie. Or maybe it's Sara. They're little strawberry-blond clones of one another.

"Not a thing," says Dr. Quinn. "They trashed the kitchen, ate some food, messed up some beds, and just left."

"Sounds like transients," says Gretchen's brother, Bob. Bob plays college tennis and so far his conversation has been pretty much limited to topspin.

"What's that?" says Sara.

"Bums."

"Bob, please." Dr. Quinn gives a small frown of disapproval as if to imply being a bum is not necessarily the bum's fault.

"Should we do anything?" says Mrs. Quinn.

Dr. Quinn shrugs. "Just make sure we turn on the alarm when we leave the house and keep our eyes open for anyone suspicious in the neighborhood."

"I'm scared," says Sara. She looks like the kind of girl who's going to be scared when it suits her for the rest of her life.

"Nothing to worry about," says Dr. Quinn. And all of a sudden there's not. Case closed, Charles in Charge. There are guys who can do this. Too bad none of them go into politics. And then it happens. Out of nowhere, Mrs. Quinn turns and looks *right at me.* "You've been awfully quiet, Billy. Is everything all right?" And now everyone's quiet and staring at me. I suddenly wonder if I've stumbled into a den of mind readers and this is a setup.

"I just like listening," I say. I take a bite of pasta. I'm no longer tasting it. My answer sounds pretty feeble, even to me.

Dr. Quinn smiles. "Just don't be afraid to jump in, son."

Son. He calls me that. It *is* the Waltons.

"I won't," I say.

The conversation moves on to the little girls asking Dr. Quinn if they can adopt a penguin and Bob telling them that the vegetable medley they're eating is flavored with hemlock, which is poisonous. The little girls shriek as if he means it.

"Who thinks it's important to be popular!?" says Dr. Quinn.

It's all so wholesome it could give you cavities. And the really crazy thing is, I like it.

35

I'm in the Quinns' backyard, sitting in their old-fashioned gazebo, when Gretchen comes out. She looks around, then sees me and comes over.

Point of reference.

A gazebo is a pavilion structure found in parks and gardens. The word is possibly derived from the Latin *videbo* meaning "I shall gaze." The Quinns' gazebo has no view but is pleasant nonetheless.

"There's ice cream if you want," Gretchen says. "Chocolate."

"I'm fine," I say. "Dinner was really good," I say.

Gretchen sits down next to me. "We talk too much," she says. You can tell she's talking about her family and she doesn't sound happy about it. "I think it's because we were together so much," says Gretchen. "You know. When we were gone?"

I realize she's talking about Africa.

"What was it like?" I say.

"We were on the Eastern Cape," Gretchen says. "We lived in Port Elizabeth. It's on the ocean. The beaches

are beautiful but the city is really ugly. Almost thirty-
five percent of the people have HIV. Mom and Dad would
go out into the country, going from township to township. A lot of times they'd take us with them. They thought
it'd give us perspective."

"Cool," I say. And it sounds like it might be.

"I hated it," says Gretchen. The quiet anger in her
voice surprises me. "I hated them for bringing us there
and making us stay so long. It was so dirty and sad. Children with *sores* played in the dirt. I mean, maybe they
can't help it, they have *nothing* but . . ."

"But what?" I say.

"I couldn't wait to get home," Gretchen says softly.
"Pretty bad, huh?"

"Pretty honest, if you ask me."

"We don't know how lucky we are, Billy," says Gretchen,
looking away. "We really don't."

I could tell her that there are those who think you make
your own luck, that there are those who believe that good
luck is a gift for benevolent works done in past lives. Better I should tell it to a little girl with sores, dying of
AIDS in Africa.

Fate. Inevitable destiny.

"But now you do know," I say. "And if you hadn't gone
to Africa maybe you wouldn't. Maybe there's a lot of
people who should go to Africa," I say. "Me, for instance.
Maybe I should go to Africa."

"No," says Gretchen, giggling. "I like you here." For a
moment she doesn't say anything else. And then she does.

"I think *we're* lucky," Gretchen says. "Because we've met each other again."

I kiss her.

It's easier this time. It's better than the first time, if it possibly can be. Her mouth is slightly open. Her lips and tongue taste faintly of ice cream. I savor it.

Fact.

Love releases the same chemicals in the brain as chocolate.

36

One of the most truly Edvard Munch's *The Scream* moments of the year has got to be Halloween. Halloween is the most horribly misinterpreted holiday in the history of the entire world.

It's also my favorite.

Partly this is because every year as long as I can remember, Mrs. Mirrens, of the broken tennis foot, throws this annual costume party, and if there is anything more stupidly hysterical than adult men and women dressing up as pirates, mermaids, lobsters, and aluminum beer cans, I don't want to know about it.

One can only laugh so much.

Mom—*Linda*—always dresses as a fair damsel or a Roman noblewoman, and I have to admit, she usually looks pretty good. Her favorite costume, though, is when she puts on slippers, silk harem pants, veils, and a little top that shows the top of her breasts. Even the fake one. She calls this costume "I Dream of Jeannie."

Historical footnote.

I Dream of Jeannie was this sitcom in the 1960s about

an astronaut who finds a bottle that contains this beautiful, sexy, two-thousand-year-old magical genie. The premise of the show is that the genie keeps sticking her breasts and butt in the astronaut's face, wanting to grant him wishes that obviously include having frantic sex with him while calling him master. Amazingly, he keeps saying no. The show can be found on Hulu, under "censored" and "unbelievable."

Actually when Mom dresses up in costumes that are kind of sexy she *is* kind of sexy, and because she is, I try not to look at her. It's undoubtedly an Oedipal thing. This, according to Freudian psychology, is the repressed desire of a guy to sexually possess his mother and kill his father. And even though the thought of having sex with Mom freaks me out completely, I must admit that every year at Halloween the thought of killing Dad does raise its head. This is because every year *Gordon* dresses as the same moron thing.

Abraham Lincoln.

Only Dad doesn't even bother to wear a costume. He puts on the same old loafers, slacks, golf shirt, and sports jacket he pretty much wears all the time and then just sticks a fake-looking black beard onto his face and chin. Not even a stovepipe hat or a mole.

"Oh, get in the spirit of things," says Mom.

"I'm not going out looking like some asshole," says Dad, not realizing that this is the whole point of an adult costume party, and besides, he already does.

Off they finally go in the Maserati, Jeannie and Mr.

Lincoln, Jeannie no doubt wishing they could stop at the Ford Theatre for an assassination before going on to the party. They'll come home after midnight spectacularly hammered and you just know questionable things have happened.

"An astronaut came on to your mother," Dad will say, trying to explain a black eye.

"Honest Abe got punched by Napoleon for trying to kiss Josephine," Mom will tell someone on the phone.

Whatever it is, they'll sleep in separate bedrooms and won't be talking to each other for several days.

Another thing I like about Halloween is that the year before she died, Dorie dressed up as the wicked, wicked witch from Oz. She painted her face green. She put on a dark dress and she put a pointed witch's hat on her head. She wore a bandana underneath it because she was bald. She grabbed a broom.

"I'll get you, my pretty! And your little dog too!"

We laughed.

And then she insisted I dress up as the Scarecrow. She told me this was typecasting because I didn't have a brain. Only straw. Out we went, me just walking with her and looking out for her, making sure she didn't get too tired as she collected candy. Then, just before going home, saving one piece for her and one piece for me, she handed all her candy out to other kids.

I still have my piece.

One of the things I don't like at Halloween is how older kids go out of their way to ruin everything. Guys go around throwing toilet paper into trees and eggs at houses, cars, and each other. Girls use it as an opportunity to dress up as whores. It's really sort of insulting because Halloween is historically a festival honoring the dead. It's a time to pray for the souls that have recently departed purgatory but have yet to reach heaven. In fact, trick-or-treating started when poor people would go door-to-door and, in exchange for food, they'd say prayers for those who'd died and passed on.

Food for prayers sounds like a good deal to me and so every Halloween I go to the store and buy huge bags of Snickers and Reese's and Jolly Ranchers, and after Mom and Dad leave, I'll turn on the yard lights and stick a chair in the driveway with the front gate open and the little kids will come in.

If the kids are too old, I ignore them.

Our neighborhood, which isn't really a neighborhood, just a collection of fancy houses, always gets a lot of poor Latino families who come from somewhere else to trick-or-treat. I guess they think our streets are a safe place to walk with their families. They'll come to the edge of the driveway and look in. The kids are shy. "Go on," the parents will say. *"Sigue."*

Their costumes are great. The little girls are almost always dressed as angels or princesses, all wings and sparkles and glitter in their dark hair. The boys are vampires and ghosts and lucha libre wrestlers.

"Wow," I'll say. "You're beautiful."

Or cool. Or scary. I'll hold out the candy bowl. And

even though it bothers me that a lot of the little Latino kids have bad teeth, some already rimmed with metal, some not even real ones, I let everyone take as much as they want.

"Go ahead. *Todo lo que quieras.*"

I do this because in return for candy I want their prayers. *Quiero tus oraciones.*

For Dorie.

37

Only this year at Halloween it rains.

38

"This is crazy!" screams Gretchen.

The smile on her face says it's not crazy at all.

With no possibility of trick-or-treaters, Gretchen has come over to the house and we have, of all things, done homework together. Which means, of course, we've accomplished absolutely nothing. The fascinating discussion of what's your favorite flavor of frozen yogurt has taken us a good hour and a half alone. The only conclusion we come to is that yogurt would not be a bad idea. We take the Jaguar and Gretchen drives. We go to Bogart Yogurt and I get something orange and Gretchen gets something pink. We trade licks.

This, of course, gives me a hard-on.

"Where to now, James?" Gretchen says, when we get back in the car. She's looking down her nose at me as if she's totally in charge. It kills me, it really does, and so I make a sort of spontaneous decision. Playing it close to the vest, I only tell her the general directions. An hour later we're only halfway there and it begins to rain harder. I ask Gretchen if she wants to turn back.

"Uh-uh," she says. I can tell she's busting with curiosity about where we're going but I keep my mouth shut. I want it to be a surprise. And it is.

"A Ferris wheel!?"

The Pacific Wheel sits at the end of Santa Monica Pier. It's the world's only solar-powered Ferris wheel, is ninety feet tall, can move eight hundred people an hour, and contains 160,000 lights.

"If you'd gone a little faster than fifty miles an hour, we might have got here yesterday," I say. I've become quite the comedian. Along with hard-ons, it seems to have come with the territory.

As I lead Gretchen by the hand down the deserted pier, it's like looking at color trails in the falling rain. Gretchen's hair and clothes are soaked. I've given her my hoodie but she's left it unzipped. She's wearing no bra and I can see her nipples poking out beneath her thin, wet top.

It *is* crazy.

I pay for the tickets. There's no line. We move up the ramp toward the spinning baskets. The attendant, wearing a rain-slick green poncho, shakes his head.

"Getting ready to shut it down," he says.

"Twenty bucks for five more minutes?" I say, and I hold out the bill. The operator takes the money. He brings the slowly spinning wheel to a halt. He opens the side door to the basket.

"Oh, I don't like heights," says Gretchen. You can tell she's thrilled.

The attendant pulls the bar down, locking us in. He

releases the gear. In a stomach-dropping surge, we move back and then up, the pier dropping away, the lights of Santa Monica coming to eye level, then dropping away as we move up toward the peak of the enormous wheel. Gretchen shrieks and buries her face in the hollow of my shoulder. Her hair is wet against my cheek and I put my arm around her shoulders. I'm laughing so hard. And then we're falling, out and down, the pier rushing up at us, only to swing in and under, past the bored attendant, past the ramp, up again and on, touched by gravity and, a moment later, weightless. As we approach the top of the wheel Gretchen looks at me in a certain way and we kiss. She tastes of rain.

A wheel is a circle. A circle is a set of points in a plane set at a fixed distance from the center. A circle is a symbol of God, whose center is everywhere and whose circumference is nowhere. A circle is a ring that symbolizes love and hope. The hope is that love will take on the characteristics of the circle and capture eternity.

On pace for the world's longest kiss, Gretchen and I come down and around and up for the third time and as we do, I reach beneath the hoodie. My fingertips lightly touch Gretchen's breasts and erect nipples. Gretchen puts her hand just beneath the junction of my thighs and presses. The moment, the world, my entire life, is a sensual blur of touch, taste, rain, and light.

39

Unlike Halloween, Thanksgiving is truly a ridiculous holiday. The world is barely tolerable and getting worse. Why give thanks? This is especially true in High School Highville where anybody who has anything thinks they deserve it and those that don't, think they deserve more.

However.

Thanksgiving is when my grandmother, Dad's mother, Beatrix, arrives for her annual visit. Beatrix is a widow, probably a lesbian, and possibly a high-functioning autistic. Her deceased husband—Dad's father, Larry—was a postman who was walking his route one day when he got run over by a garbage truck. The truck was backing up and didn't see Larry. Larry was reading someone's mail and didn't see the truck. Beatrix never remarried. She trained and then took a job as a clerk to a judge in Fresno, California, which is where Dad grew up. She refers to the judge as the judicial train wreck, the pinheaded halfwit, and the alcoholic slug. She's been writing his decisions now for over twenty years.

Beatrix is tall and thin with short white hair, never wears makeup, and is totally oblivious to what she wears. She speaks in a flat voice devoid of inflection, rarely smiles and if she does it's this tiny, sort of self-amused little wrinkle. I've never seen her laugh. She doesn't give a crap about what people think, she'll say exactly what she thinks about anything and anyone at a moment's notice, and she's always leaving the room for no apparent reason, usually when somebody else is talking.

She's just great.

"Your idea of clean," she'll say to the housekeeper, "would make a zookeeper blanch."

"Your father was a complacent boob," she'll say to Dad. "Try not to take after him *too* much."

Beatrix does try to be nice to Mom. I think she knows that Mom has been through a lot. "You're a lovely, well-meaning woman," she'll say. "But unless you want to live the rest of your life as a borderline hysteric, you should be in therapy twice a week." She's not being critical. She just calls it the way she sees it.

I enjoy Beatrix. I always sense that like me, she's on the outside looking in, but unlike me, she's not so much dismayed as she is exasperated by what she sees. The world would be a better place if she was writing the decisions for everyone.

Another thing I like is that Beatrix is always asking me what I'm reading, and when I tell her, chances are she's already read it.

"*Martin Eden* by Jack London," I'll say.

"The story of a disdainful drudge who thinks the world revolves totally around him," Beatrix will say.

"It's called individualism," I'll say.

"It's called nonsense. An egotist so filled with life he has no other option but to kill himself. And then the idiot actually *does* it by jumping off a ship in the middle of the ocean. After making self-aggrandizing speeches for a good half hour, he finally goes down and good riddance to him."

"Gee, now I don't have to finish it."

Beatrix also tells me about books that she thinks *I* should be reading. *"Brideshead Revisited.* Explores the act of love by which God calls souls to Himself. Written in 1945 by Evelyn Waugh, who at the age of twenty-three, in a fit of homosexual panic, *also* decided it would be a good idea to drown himself. According to him, he was talked out of it by a jellyfish."

"Good thing that jellyfish didn't run into Martin Eden."

Beatrix's lips don't smile, but her eyes do.

"Indeed."

Beatrix has a photographic memory.

I do too.

Beatrix knows a little bit, sometimes quite a lot, about everything.

I do too.

Which sometimes makes me wonder if I'm not a high-functioning autistic lesbian. Anything's possible though I don't think Beatrix lies awake nights unable to sleep.

Fact.

Thanksgiving dinner is a disaster.

"I think it'd be nice if everyone individually gave thanks for something," says Mom when we sit down at the dinner table.

"The 49ers's are ahead at the end of the half," says Gordon, pouring from a bottle of expensive champagne. You can see Mom's jaw clench. The San Francisco 49ers are Dad's favorite football team. By telling us the game's at halftime, Dad's letting us know dinner will be over, at least for him, at the beginning of the third quarter.

We eat. The housekeeper has prepared this massive turkey with all the trimmings with the idea that there will be leftovers. And there will be a lot of leftovers because nobody at the table really *likes* turkey. Or *aligot* mashed potatoes. Or French green beans with caramelized onions. Or pomegranate-cranberry relish. Or a field-greens salad in a white balsamic dressing with crushed, toasted walnuts. Dad might if they were all deep fried.

"It's the tradition," says Mom.

"Meaning what?" says Dad, checking his watch.

"Meaning the Pilgrims ate it," says Mom, trying to smile.

"Pilgrims wouldn't have known a green bean if they shit one," says Dad. "Pilgrims mostly starved to death."

"Mmm, this is great," I say, my mouth full. Storm clouds are gathering and I'm trying to head them off at the pass. "Thanks a lot for Happy Thanks-a-lot-giving!"

It doesn't work.

"Well, Gordon," says Beatrix, pushing oyster stuffing

around her plate, "I suppose you're still dressing right these days." Totally out of nowhere. As if she's been saving it up.

"Dressing left" and "dressing right" are terms used by tailors when fitting suit pants. It refers to the direction a man's balls sag in relation to the zipper and for some reason is Beatrix's way of discussing politics. She seems to feel that liberal or conservative is totally based on which way your dick points.

It's as good a reason as any.

Dad, of course, began dressing solidly right around the same time he realized he had money. Before that he was a member of the "go away and leave me the fuck alone" party. Actually I suppose they're one and the same thing.

"We don't talk politics at the dinner table," says Dad.

This is because, unlike Gordon, Mom is a liberal who cares about immigrants, war orphans, homeless people, social services, and puppies. I'm not sure if this means Mom's left breast is slightly bigger than the other but, regardless, Mom and Dad are always getting into arguments over politics, especially when Dad points out that although Mom says she cares about all these things, she doesn't do anything about them, not even vote.

"It appears to me," says Beatrix, "you don't talk about *anything* at the dinner table."

"What would *you* like to talk about, Bea?" says Mom. She's looking more and more nervous and upset. She really wants holidays to go well, which is why they usually don't.

"Why don't we talk about how many times I've asked you not to call me that," says Beatrix.

"You're right, I apologize," says Mom.

"You apologize too much," says Beatrix. "You either don't mean it or you have identity issues. Which is it?"

"Gordon," says Mom. "May I speak to you in the kitchen?"

"No," says Gordon. Which is his way of saying he's not going to touch this with a ten-foot pole. To which Mom gets up and leaves the table and comes back five minutes later with her eyes red. To which Dad leaves the table and comes back ten minutes later with a half-consumed bottle of Willamette Valley pinot noir. To which Mom leaves the table again and this time doesn't come back at all. To which Gordon takes his wine into the family room, where no one ever gathers, to watch football.

"Our family is very odd, Billy," says Beatrix, as she wipes her mouth with her napkin. "I doubt you'll find much to be amused with in life unless you make it happen yourself."

"What are your thoughts on breaking into strangers' houses?"

It might be my imagination but I think I detect another one of Beatrix's small smiles. "Knock twice to make sure no one's home."

I go over to Gretchen's house just in time to see San Francisco lose in the fourth quarter.

40

We go over the wall. The house looks expensive from the outside. All stucco and glass. I knock twice, then EZ-pick the lock and push the side door to the kitchen open. We're good at this now. Ephraim moves to the beeping security system and punches in the codes. I move to the phone to wait for the call, if it comes. Twom and Deliza move quickly into the kitchen. It's only when we turn on a light that we realize it's a pigsty. Drawers and cupboards are open. Open cans, milk and juice bottles, and Chinese takeout cartons are on the counters. There are unwashed pans on the stove. The sink is full of grimy dishes and there is the smell of rotting food.

"Maybe the maid didn't come," says Ephraim, weakly.

"Billy?" We hear Twom call from the other room and we move to join him. He and Deliza stand in the entryway to the living room.

"Whoa . . ." says Ephraim.

It is beyond badly decorated. Ashtrays overflow. Carpets are soiled. Wine bottles, glasses, and junk are everywhere.

It's as if hyenas live in this house.

"Maybe it's a rental," says Ephraim.

"Maybe you're an idiot," says Deliza. "Choosing a house like this."

"I didn't *know*," pleads Ephraim.

We don't split up. We move as a group, going from room to room. Beds are unmade. Sheets are stained. You wouldn't lie down for fear of what you might come up with. The bathrooms reek. Discarded clothes and trash are everywhere. There are no computers. There are no photo albums. There is no art on the wall, just faded paint where something once might have hung. The bookshelves are completely empty.

Maybe no one lives here. Maybe even now they're running to save themselves.

"Billy."

It's Twom. I hadn't realized he left us. He has a look on his face I've never seen before. He takes us to what in another house might be the maid's quarters.

No. Someone lives in this house. Monsters live here. Grendel lives here.

The room smells of piss and shit. Vials of pills, chips, boxes of cold cereal and crackers, and an empty half-gallon bottle of Coke are on the bedside tables.

The old woman's eyes are rheumy. Her thinning hair, the scabs on her scalp, her nightclothes, her bedding—all are beyond sickening. Her skin is green parchment. You can see where she's scratched herself with her ragged nails. Her mouth works. Opens and closes, opens and closes. Like a sucker fish. She makes no sound.

I see a cell phone on the side table. Well beyond the old woman's reach. Using a napkin, I pick it up. I put the phone on speaker. I don't want to get it any closer to my mouth than I have to.

The firemen are the first to arrive. Then the paramedics. The cops come last. We've turned on the alarms before we left, When they force their way in, they go off. A few minutes of it and then neighbors come out onto the street to see what's going on. We join them.

We watch when the medics wheel the old woman out of the house. Her eyes are closed now. She looks asleep. Or dead. I hear somebody whisper to someone else that the woman's caregivers, a married Russian couple hired by her children, often take off for the weekend. What's a few days alone to someone who has no sense of time and never comes out of their room?

41

I've come in the house and am heading toward the stairs when I hear Dad call me.

"Billy? Billy, is that you?"

Dad—*Gordon*—is sitting on the couch in the living room. Like me, he also watches TV with the sound off. Maybe it's a genetic thing. There is a glass and a bottle of expensive, single-malt Scotch in front of him. Two thirds of it are gone.

Fact.

A functioning alcoholic is able to maintain a seemingly normal life, all while drinking alcoholically. He is often in denial as to his drinking as are his friends and loved ones. He thinks that drinking expensive wine or spirits means he is not alcoholic. He drinks habitually. He drinks compulsively. He drinks alone.

"Where you been?" says Dad, alone and drinking.

"I've been to a place where parents, when they grow old, are put into the hands of people who don't know or care about them," I say. "A place where cards that are no longer in play are thrown into the discard pile."

I don't say that.

"Just out."

"Still seeing that girl, huh?"

"Her name's Gretchen." I shouldn't have to remind him.

"I'd jump on that if I were you," says Dad. He sort of grins as he says it, so I'll know he's joking. I couldn't have imagined the evening getting any worse but, joke or not, the thought of my father jumping on Gretchen makes it official. At that moment I really dislike him and I turn to leave the room.

"Wait a sec."

When I turn back, Dad is looking me and he looks sad. "Billy, I—kiddo, that was . . . out of line. Little too much of the ol' whisky-doodle here." *Whisky-doodle.* He actually calls it that. And then, just when you think he *really* can't make it any more terrible, he does. "Know the worst part about getting old, kiddo? Regret. Things you should have done, things you shouldn't have. Even with all this . . ." Dad gestures vaguely around the room. "I just always thought . . ." He trails off.

"You don't *do* anything!" I yell, suddenly furious at him. "You have no job or hobby! You have no friends! You have no reason to live!"

I don't say a word.

Dad stares into space a moment. He sighs. When he looks back at me it's like he's surprised to still find me there. He makes himself smile.

"Just always remember I love you, okay?"

What kills me at this moment is that I know he does.

And the thing is, I love him too. Maybe the old woman's kids loved her once as well.

"Okay," I say.

"G'night, kiddo. Sleep well."

"I will."

But I won't. Nightmares have followed me home. I can't help but picture myself old and alone someday, sucking on my tongue as if it's a pacifier. Sleep is out of the question. I go downstairs to the drum room, and accompanied by the Reverend Tholomew Plague, I thrash far into the night.

42

This is the day at the end of the first semester that Twom and I get our report cards. The two of us get straight Cs. For different reasons, we're both incredibly proud of ourselves and each other.

43

Maybe it's just my opinion but Christmas is the absolute worst time of year imaginable, it really, truly, totally, completely, fucking is.

First of all, about a billion innocent trees get turned into mulch so that mail worldwide can get bogged down with Christmas cards from people you don't know, don't think about, and who don't know or think about you the other 364 days of the year. As a matter of fact, that's why they're usually photo cards of the entire family so you can be reminded what they look like. Mom puts them on the refrigerator. Dad throws them unopened into the wastebasket. On this, I'm with Dad.

Second of all, Christmas decorations start going up right after Thanksgiving. In our neighborhood, it's like a corporate competition to see who can throw the most blinking, blistering lights up on the outside of their palatial house. This is not to mention the reindeer, stars, Santa's sleighs, plastic snowmen, full-blown nativity scenes, and giant menorahs they set up on their lawns. Most people hire *workers* to do it. And then, just like on All

Hallows' Eve, people from the less affluent communities, entire extended families of them, come and drive up and down the street, totally stupefied that people anywhere could foot this kind of megawatt electric bill.

But what really kills me is that nobody knows what the decorations even *mean* anymore. They don't know the star is a sign of a prophecy fulfilled, that God has supposedly sent us his Son, the Hope and Light of mankind. They have no idea that tree ornaments reflect this light, that their color is His blood and that green symbolizes everlasting life. The needles of evergreen trees point to heaven. Bells guide lost sheep back to the fold and the candy cane, the Shepards' crook, herds them. The ribbons tell us we're all tied together, and the wreath, another circle, also green, is the symbol of never-ending love.

~~Subjective opinion.~~

Christmas has become nothing more than an excuse to shop. Right after Thanksgiving and sometimes before, Mom and her tennis buddies, all of whom consider bargain hunting a blood sport, start buying gifts right and left for everybody, and in an incredible display of stamina, keep on going till the twenty-fourth. Dad, on the other hand, heads out at, like, ten o'clock on Christmas Eve, usually to get something for Mom and me not because he wants to but because he has to. And he has no idea what to get either of us and always comes home with a mountain of useless shit. One year he got Mom car tires, a twelve-gauge shotgun, and as a joke, a one-way, first-class ticket to Uzbekistan, the only doubly landlocked country in Central Asia. Mom, who was not amused, returned the gun and tires and got a cash refund on the ticket. Which she kept.

Really, it's like everybody is supposed to get something even if they don't need or deserve it. Especially kids. It's not about you being naughty or nice, it's about how many bucks your parents can afford to spend. You can be good and get nothing because your parents are cheap or poor bastards, which means, to a little kid, that they've been bad. And then there are people like Deliza and John Montebello, who get buried in expensive gifts. Which leads them to believe they can get away with anything for the rest of their lives.

It goes without saying more people are arrested, placed in mental institutions, or commit suicide at Christmas than any other time of year. And frankly, a padded room would be preferable to our house because worse than the decorations, the cards, and the gifts, Christmas is when Mom's folks, Frank and Lorna, come and stay for a week.

Frank and Lorna are both the children of Oakies who moved from Oklahoma to California in the 1930s. "Oakies" is another word for poor, uneducated white trash and it's pretty much agreed that their moving to California increased the average intelligence of both states.

Frank, who's a retired electrical lineman, is the kind of guy neighbors turn to. If you were marooned on a deserted island, he'd have a house with running water built out of palm fronds in, like, two minutes. And by the time he finished, Lorna would have dinner ready.

Frank, who never trims his nose hair, will go around the house, looking for anything that's loose, dirty, dull, broken, needs to be oiled, sharpened, sanded, painted, tightened, or fixed, and not finding anything, will then go hop on the lawn mower and cut the grass in the backyard. By the end of the week, the grass is begging for him to leave. And even though we have a housekeeper, Lorna will make beds, do laundry, iron, vacuum, and do dishes. By the end of the week, the housekeeper will be begging her to leave.

But the real problem is this. Frank and Lorna take all these semiredeeming qualities and then they screw them up by being morons. In fact, Frank and Lorna are *proud* to be morons.

"Too much education makes people think they're better than regular folks," they'll say.

"Regular folks don't get their money for free."

"Immigrants are taking jobs away from *real* Americans,"

"Global warming hasn't been proven. It's just words."

"We go our own pace in traffic." As if they're proud to inconvenience people.

"All it takes is common sense and good character." "It's nothing but Jew talk." "Homosexuals *choose* to be what they are." Not to mention my favorite—

"Parenting isn't easy, Linda, just look at Billy."

It makes me feel like a member of the starship *Enterprise* listening to Klingons without the help of a universal translator.

"We *work* for a living."

But they don't. Frank lost whatever meager pension he had when the housing bubble burst and he and Lorna live on Social Security and generous handouts from Mom and Dad. And thanks to Medicare, the doctor's office is a big part of their social life. They like to have their urine checked and their blood drawn on a weekly basis because it's an opportunity to catch up on current periodicals, not to mention hobnob with all their other medically challenged friends. Frank and Lorna consider lunch in a hospital cafeteria a date.

But the very worst thing of all at Christmas is this. Frank and Lorna believe that Dorie dying was, in its own way, a blessing. We'll be opening all these stupid presents on Christmas morning—Frank and Lorna always give gift cards from Walmart because they want to make sure we *get something we really want*—and Mom, who still hangs Dorie's stocking on the mantel every Christmas, will start getting teary-eyed because Dorie isn't there.

"Now, sweetheart," Frank will say, "you know she's in a better place."

"The moment she left us, she was at the foot of our Savior," says Lorna. "She's keeping a spot warm for the rest of us."

They say this to Mom because they think it will make her feel better. Maybe they even believe it. But Mom doesn't care about heaven, all she wants is Dorie there on the couch next to her, and so all it does is make Mom cry harder. Which makes Dad break out the Bloody Marys.

Which makes me so quietly angry, I want to banish Frank and Lorna to the starship *Enterprise* and see how *they* like spending Christmas with aliens. Really, all I want for Christmas is for Frank and Lorna to take their well-intentioned stupidity home and never in a million years come back. It just all sucks, it really does, and I wish for Mom's sake and maybe even Dad's, it was better.

I flee the asylum and spend late Christmas afternoon at Gretchen's house. I'm not expecting much but I'm surprised. All they have is a small, simple Christmas tree. It's in a pot so it can be replanted. The rule in Gretchen's house is that each person in the family buys just one gift to give to another family member. Because Gretchen and her family have Christmas dinner on Christmas Eve before they go to serve food in a soup kitchen we eat leftovers. Red pepper soup. Spinach and mushroom pie. Vegetarian meat loaf. Roasted brie with cranberry dressing. Pilgrims would hate it.

Afterward, the Quinns break out this game called Trivial Pursuit which is all about answering pointless questions. Not thinking, I win the game in a landslide.

Gretchen has gotten me three sets of ProMark Hickory 747 "Rock" Wood drumsticks. She's put them all together and wrapped them so I have no idea what they are at first.

"I think they're your favorites."

They are. It's truly an excellent gift.

I get Gretchen a little gold pin. It takes me weeks to find it, and when I do it's in a used jewelry store. It doesn't look like much. It's bloodstone—green, dotted with small red spots. According to legend bloodstone was first formed when drops of Christ's blood fell from the Cross and stained some jasper, which is a form of silica. I don't believe any of it for a second but the green matches Gretchen's eyes and contrasts beautifully with her hair. She touches my face when I give it her. She kisses me before she opens it. She cries when she sees it. She tells me it's the most beautiful gift she's ever gotten in her life.

It's impossible that there are people like this in the world. I don't trust it. But that doesn't mean I don't sort of enjoy it.

44

"Hah! The Night Visitors!" says Ephraim.

We're sitting on a tiled deck by an enormous pool. Behind us, the rear of the house is all paneled glass and white stucco. Across the pool and out beyond the expanse of lawn, life-sized, cast-bronze sculptures of two winged horses, cactus garden, and high, white wall, the cliff drops thirty feet down a seawall to the rocks and sand. Beyond the sand is the Pacific Ocean. Out somewhere beyond the ocean are the radioactive remains of Japan.

The house is owned by an acquaintance of Deliza's father. Deliza says her mother, *la reina de discreción*, has intimated the guy's a high-ranking member of a Mexican drug cartel and that Deliza's father launders money and deposits it in Stateside banks for him. Deliza says she knows for a fact that he and his family are hardly ever there, that the place is left empty for months at a time, and that the front gate into the courtyard is always left unlocked.

"Why should we sneak into the place," I say, "when it sounds like all we need is your father's permission to visit?"

"It's not that kind of relationship," Deliza says. "My father's scared to death of him."

"If your father's afraid of him, maybe we should be too?" I say.

"Grow some balls, Billy," Deliza says.

"You don't have any," I say, "and you seem pretty fearless."

It's put to a vote and I lose three to one. This is happening more and more lately. Twom and Deliza are a team and Ephraim always sides with Twom.

I'm not sure I like democracy.

We park the Mercedes two blocks north of the house. Even in a community of high-priced, beachfront real estate, Casa de Esperanza stands out like an albino elephant at the zoo. Wearing shorts and T-shirts and flip-flops and carrying towels, we walk south as if going to the beach. When we get to the house, we quickly push the gate open, turn into the stone courtyard, and move around to the side of the house. I have the EZ pick, Ephraim has the security code. We don't need either one. The door is open and the security system isn't turned on.

The house is not just deserted, it is next to empty.

There is a grand piano, a couch, and a single chair, all covered with white sheets, in the cavernous living room. There is a long, dust-covered table but no chairs in the dining room. There are no rugs on the hardwood floors. No books in the bookcases. No brooms in the broom closet. There are no computers, no televisions, no photos.

There are two cans of Tecate beer and a tiny ice-encrusted pizza in the fridge.

"No wonder they never visit," says Twom.

That this monstrous, multimillion-dollar oceanfront house is unused seems almost sacrilegious and I make a mental note to post an ad in the local weekly or maybe Craigslist, telling people it's open and available to squatters. The truth is, I've come to resent houses that are not homes. I don't like it when things feel unused or fake, when the furniture is draped with artificial animal hides and the books on the shelves aren't even real, just leather-bound decorations, the author and titles printed on the spine in gold filigree, nothing inside but blank pages. Even cavemen painted their caves with items and drawings that reflected their lives.

This cave is dead.

With nothing else to do, we have adjourned to the pool. The filter is on a daily timer and the water is pristine and clear. Deliza and Twom are playing backgammon at a poolside table. Ephraim and I are lying on deck chairs with cushions but no covers. I have a biography of George Washington that I've brought along as "beach reading." Beatrix sent it to me and I'm starting to think it's her idea of a joke. In skimming it, I've already learned that the favorite foods of of our country's father were mashed sweet potatoes with coconut, string beans with mushrooms, cream of peanut soup, salt cod, and—cue the Ebonics—hoecakes. Washington lost all of his teeth cracking Brazil nuts with his jaws. Washington wore dentures made out of a hippopotamus tusk. They hurt so much he used opium to alleviate the pain. He snored like a champ, had a speech impediment, and like Twom, was probably dyslexic. For pretty much his entire life, he owned slaves.

Sounds like the father of our country to me.

"The what?" says Twom. He is shirtless and drinking the beer from the fridge. His tattoos glisten under a sheen of sweat.

"The Night Visitors," Ephraim says again. Ephraim is reading a local newspaper—probably a first for him—pinched from in front of a neighbor's house. Imitating Twom, he's taken off his shirt and his pale worm of a body is already pink and glowing, on the verge of being sunburned to death.

"Who are night visitors?" says Twom, as if whoever they are, they're morons.

"We are. That's what they're calling us," says Ephraim. He's excited about it. "Listen, listen." He begins to read out loud. "'Law enforcement officers emphasize that the night visitors don't appear to be stealing. So far their criminal behavior hasn't gone beyond empty refrigerators and re-formatted home computers.'"

"Reformatted?" says Twom.

"I wonder who did that." Deliza sneers.

"You're a shithead, Ephraim," I say. I'm truly disgusted. Since what I now refer to as the Night of the Desolate Woman, it seems important that we leave things better than when we arrived. I've started making beds, cleaning up the kitchen, and leaving money for food before we exit a house.

"It's my calling card," Ephraim says, only a little defensive. He continues reading. "'Nevertheless, this unlawful activity is unsettling and potentially dangerous. Community residents should take proper security measures and report any gardeners, domestics, and tradespeople they don't recognize in their neighborhoods.'"

"Sure," says Deliza, "blame the Mexicans."

Ephraim looks up, suddenly worried.

"It says they have a number of leads."

No one says anything. Till now, I don't think it's occurred to any of us that we could actually ever get caught.

"What kind of leads?" I say.

"It doesn't give any details," says Ephraim.

"Ah, then it's all bullshit," Twom says. "If they knew anything, they'd do something about it. Besides, what are they gonna do, throw us in jail for drinking their beer?" He raises the can of Tecate and drains it.

"You tell'm, baby," says Deliza. She throws the dice, scores doubles, and counts the last of her pieces off the board. Twom stares down at the board as if uncertain as to what just happened. Rising, Deliza stretches like a cat. And now, out of nowhere, probably because nowhere is ~~probably~~ where her mind lives and works most of the time, she begins to undress.

"What are you doing?" says Twom. But he's smiling as if he knows exactly what she's doing.

"Getting naked. Billy doesn't care and Ephraim would

rather you take off *your* pants." Deliza looks at Ephraim.
"*¿Verdad?*" She says it in this sweet, high-pitched voice
that makes her sound like she's a blameless little girl.

"Shut up," says Ephraim.

"Ooh, you so tough," says Deliza. She drops her bra on
Ephraim's head.

"Come on, huh!" Ephraim tosses the bra aside. His
face looks scalded.

Stripping off her thong panties, Deliza lies down on a
lounge chair directly across from me. I'm staring. I don't
want to, it feels disloyal to Gretchen, but I can't help it.
Pictures and porno clips don't prepare you for flesh and
blood. Deliza's skin is mocha colored. Her breasts are
larger than Gretchen's, the nipples are dark and erect. She
wears a small gold ring in her navel. She has no tan lines.
She has shaved all her pubic hair and her sex seems puffy
and engorged.

You suddenly know it wasn't just a face that launched
a thousand ships.

I look away. I pretend to read about George Washington, but out of the corner of my eye, I can't help but continue to look.

And she knows it.

45

It's the sound of a car door slamming and it makes me stop breathing.

I have left George Washington and Deliza's labia, have gone into the house, crossed the empty living room, gone up the stairs, moved down the hall, and turned into a bedroom where, lying down on a sheetless, coverless, pillowless mattress, I have tried to sleep. Even though my brain is aching and I'm running on fumes, it's impossible.

This house has its own personal nightmares.

I quickly jump up and off the mattress. As I come out of the bedroom I hear the sound of a metal gate opening. When I move to the window at the top of the stairs to peek out, I see that a home security car is parked out on the street and that a uniformed, armed guard is crossing the courtyard toward the front door. I see that a second guard is out on the street. It hits me all at once that we left the gate swinging open.

Doomsday rolling in my gut, I run down the hall. I race down the stairs and through the foyer. I run into and across the living room. I run out the open doors into the back, toward the pool. The image of a howler monkey, mouth agape, screaming a warning, flashes across my brain. I throw a cupped hand over the monkey's open mouth.

No one is there.

No Ephraim, no Twom, no naked Deliza. There are no beer cans, no backgammon set, no clothes, no towels. The sun shines. The sea is white and shimmering. Or is it a desert I'm looking at? Maybe I *am* asleep. It's come to this. I'm so snooze deprived, I can no longer distinguish sleep from awake, dream state from reality.

The sound of the doorbell is all the wake-up I need. It sends me racing back into the house. In the living room, I detour into the adjoining dining room where the abandoned table lives. I move through the far doorway and enter into a hallway. Moving down the hallway I pass a rear stairway that climbs to the second floor. I keep going. Moving past the pantry with its endless empty shelves, I hear voices.

In the industrial-sized kitchen, Twom and Deliza are just putting the frozen pizza into the microwave oven. I'm hyperventilating so badly, I can hardly speak. They look at me, alarmed.

I start breathing again. Barely.

"Guards . . . security . . ."

"We're out of here," Twom says, and he grabs Deliza by the arm and turns for the door. I start to follow. I stop.

"Where's Ephraim?"

Twom looks back in surprise. "He went with you."

"Does it look like he went with me!" I say.

"Leave him," says Deliza. "He can take care of himself."

"Are you off the edge?" I say.

"Are *you?*" says Deliza.

"He'll tell them everything," I say.

"Aw, shit," says Twom. What else is there to say? All of us know that it's true. Maybe he's already confessing. I ask myself, other than the legal fees, the court appearances, the notoriety and the shame, what's the worst that can happen? I'm a clean-cut, well-spoken white kid whose parents have money. I've never been in trouble before and my future is bright. I promise myself that after I get out of prison, where I'll no doubt be serially sodomized into oblivion by large, angry men, I will never do stupid things again.

"Go," I say. "I'll find him."

To his credit, Twom hesitates for a brief moment. "We'll meet you at the car." And then he and Deliza are out the door and gone.

I turn and run out of the kitchen. I run through the pantry and back down the hall past the stairs. I run into the dining room. I'm just about to run into the living room when something stops me. I stop and I peek around the door frame and across toward the foyer like some dumb kid playing kick the can.

Olly-olly-oxen-free! All come home!

I wish.

I hear the key turn in the front door lock. I see the door open a crack, then open all the way. The security guard is about fifty years old, with a belly that hangs over his wide black belt. He moves to the alarm system which, of course, is off.

I retreat. I tiptoe back across the dining room and down the hallway. I get to the back stairs leading to the second floor. I want to get out of here, I want to join Twom and Deliza at the car. I want to go home. Instead, I go up the stairs two at a time. I'm at the second-floor landing when Ephraim crashes bodily into me. We bang into the wall and fall in a heap.

"There are people!" gasps Ephraim. He's lost his glasses in the fall and is bug-eyed with fear.

"No kidding, shut up!" I'm ready to hit him in his stupid, pale, moron face, I really am. "They're security guards," I say.

"Oh, my God, oh, my God," says Ephraim. "What do we do?"

I want to tell him that God has better things to do than come to the rescue of a pimple-faced, junk-food-eating reformatter of hard drives but I don't. "We be quiet and we hide," I say. Fat chance. Ephraim is already beginning to burble like a baby. And now, wouldn't you know it, his asthma kicks in.

Fact.

Asthma is a chronic disease, its chief characteristic being inflammation in the airways. The throat muscles tighten and the lining of the air passages swells. The amount of air taken in is dramatically reduced. Asthma can be triggered by anxiety or panic.

Translation.

Since anxiety and panic are Ephraim's two middle names, in a matter of micromoments he is a wheezing, choking lump of worthless protoplasm. I have no choice. I pull Ephraim up. I kick, pull, punch, and half carry and half drag him down the hall. I push Ephraim into a bed-room.

"Get under the bed," I say, "and stay there."

Ephraim nods. He's blinking tears. Snot is coming from his nose. He's wheezing like an old man getting ready to die. As he crawls under the bed, I can hear some-one coming up the front staircase.

"Hello? Anybody up there?"

Ephraim sobs and coughs and farts and covers his stupid mouth and nose and sobs and coughs again. No way I'm getting under a bed with him.

"Anybody here?" calls the voice again. I hear the creak of footsteps at the top of the stairs.

It goes like this.

Ephraim is babbling incoherently as the two of us, hands cuffed behind us, are led out of the house by the home security guards.

"They made me I didn't want to it wasn't my idea at all it was all his Billy Kinsey Billy his father is Gordon Kinsey and his mother is Linda and the others are Wil-lard Twomey and Deliza Baraza who made me they're to blame not me I didn't reformat any hard drives!"

Of course, this doesn't happen. There is only one way it can really go.

I pull Ephraim out from under the bed and up off the floor. "Get up!" I say. "Move, move!" Turning, I run Ephraim across the bedroom toward the paned glass window. He screams as we go crashing through.

In a rain of glass and wood, we fall. Ephraim is still screaming but I can't hear him. I feel mildly surprised and resigned at what I've done. It's twenty feet down and we land badly on the cement. My legs twist one way, my body another. Ephraim's head strikes the ground and bounces, then hits again. We tumble and roll and come to rest. We don't get up.

A seagull caws.

I'm on my back. There is blood in my mouth. The angle of my spine tells me my back is broken. I turn my head. Ephraim's face is inches away. His eyes are open and blankly staring. I turn my head and look up into the pistol of the second guard.

"Am I gone 'rest you?" he says with a redneck Southern accent. "Or you gonna die 'n' save me the trouble?"

Fortunately an option other than these presented itself.

The guard is about halfway down the hall, when I come out of the bedroom, pulling my T-shirt over my head. I cough slightly. When I see the guard, see the gun in his hand, I cry out and pull back in fear. I hope I'm not dealing with an amateur, some custodian trying to pick up a few bucks in his spare time.

"Don't hurt me!" I say. "Please!"

"Don't move," the guard says. He looks nervous. He lowers the pistol only slightly as he takes the walkie-talkie off his utility belt. "I have somebody upstairs," the guard says. He stares at me again. "Kid, you want to tell me what you're doing here?"

"I'm staying here?" I say, making it a question.

"Here?" says the guard. He sounds skeptical.

"For the weekend?" I say. "I'm on break? From USC? I mean, it was supposed to be okay."

The guard speaks into his walkie-talkie again. "Hold on," he says. He looks at me again. "Do the Esperanzas know you're here?"

"Well, yeah," I say. "I mean, like, my mom set it up. She and Mrs. Esperanza are really good friends. And the groundskeeper left the side door open for me and they gave me the code for the alarm. I can give it to you if you want." I try to look worried. "Or if you want you can call my mom?"

The guard looks uncertain.

"Brigham?" he says into his walkie-talkie. "Come on up."

Ten minutes later, I'm at the front door bidding both of them a fond farewell. As security personnel go, they're downright friendly.

"Sorry for the scare, *Mr. Montebello*," the older guard says.

"No, it's okay. Really," I say. "It's really good that you were doing your job. Really." I wonder if I should tip them.

"If you go out, make sure to reset the alarm, sir," the younger guard says. The fact that I know the code has made a huge difference. As has the fact that the Esperanzas are in Mexico, probably in hiding from other drug cartels, and can't be reached for verification.

"I will," I say. "Thanks! Have a great day!"

The older guard actually waves as they drive out the gate. It really sort of sucks that if I was a black, punk homeboy I'd be in the back of the car with him. Or even dead. But I'm a clean-cut, well-spoken, white kid in cargo shorts and a polo shirt. And he wasn't a custodian trying to make a few bucks on the side.

He was a moonlighting schoolteacher.

46

Deliza's Mercedes is on the street where we left it. I'm almost surprised. Twom would want to wait but after twenty minutes Deliza would no doubt want to get the hell out of Dodge, leaving us to fend for ourselves. Most of the time lately in an argument like this, she wins.

Ephraim and I approach at a fast walk. Ephraim is still huffing and heaving. Getting him out of the house was like lifting and carrying a long toothpaste tube of blubbering mucus. If anyone had stopped and asked, I'd already decided to tell them I've just saved Ephraim from drowning. And in a way, I have.

"Billy, what the fuck, dude," says Twom.

"Just get us out of here," I say. "I am so over this."

"Yeah, but what happened?" Twom says. "You okay?"

I push Ephraim into the back of the Benz. "Everything's fine. Just get us home, will you?" I'm trying not to yell. I know from having to listen to Dad all the time that when you yell, people don't really listen to you, even if you're right. And so I'm really trying hard not to scream.

"Please," I say, very quietly. "Let's all go home. We'll talk about it later."

The whole way, Ephraim never opens his eyes and never stops whimpering. "Never. Never again," he says. "Never, never, ever again." It's cringe inducing that he's such a wuss but I'm pretty much thinking the same thing myself.

"Billy."

Twom is looking at me in the rearview mirror.

"Did they see you? See your face?"

I nod. Maybe it's why they let me off. They felt sorry for the scared-looking kid with the easy-to-describe, one-of-a-kind, deep purple hemangioma on the side of his face.

47

"Something's different," says Dr. Quinn as if he's not sure exactly what it is. Killer Cover Total Blockout is a theatrical makeup, a makeup for *actors*—meaning people pretending to be what they're not. I've pretty much started wearing a light base of it twenty-four-seven. You can hardly see the stain on my cheek unless you look close.

I'm at the Quinns' because it's Valentine's Day. Mom and Dad have driven me over and dropped me off because I'm taking Gretchen out to dinner. They've actually decided to go do something romantic as well. Something romantic. They say that. At least Mom does. Dad has set us up at his favorite restaurant. He's called in his credit card, told the manager to take care of us, told me to order Gretchen anything she wants. He's insisted I borrow one of his sports jackets, and even though it's way too big, I can tell he's getting a kick out of being Joe-Dad, and so I take it. It's black cashmere and it doesn't look too bad.

"You're so handsome," Mom keeps saying. I get the impression she's sort of pleased that I've started using Killer Cover. Not that she would ever have *suggested* it, but since it's *my* decision, she thinks it's a good thing. Mom likes it that I might be handsome.

Gretchen looks beautiful. She's wearing high heels and this short, slim-fitting dress. Her legs are ridiculously long and sculptured from all the running she does. Her red hair is brushed out all straight and smooth. She's wearing makeup that brings out her eyes and she has on some kind of pale lip gloss. When you get right down to it, it's ridiculous that she's with me.

Gretchen drives her dad's van. It takes us about an hour to find a parking place in the village, and it's at least a ten-minute walk to the restaurant but it's the best part of the evening so far because we hold hands the entire time. Gretchen has long fingers and beautifully shaped nails. She doesn't paint them.

The restaurant is this elegant place with tablecloths where the maître d' escorts you to your table and a busboy immediately puts butter on your side plate. As the maître d' hands you a menu, a waiter, who does *not* introduce himself, asks if you want sparkling or flat water. Either way, you know it's going to cost extra.

The cheapest entrée on the menu is about a billion dollars, and each item has a paragraph underneath written in fake, flowing script that tells you where the ingredients came from and who produced it, as if knowing where the broccoli is grown and the salmon is caught and what ranch raised and butchered the beer-fed cow will make it all taste better. The paragraph goes on to explain in meticulous detail how each moist, succulent, tender, fragrant dish is grilled, braised, sautéed, smoked, poached, or roasted and describes the effluences, zests, herbs, oils, shavings, garnishes, and sauces that complete the dish. Everything is à la carte, all sides cost another zillion dollars, and if we were old enough, for another ninety bucks each we could do a specially selected wine tasting with the meal. All in all, the place is terrible and filled with old people and Gretchen and I last about a minute and a half.

We go down the street to a Thai restaurant. Gretchen gets a vegetarian pad Thai and I get some shrimp fried rice. We share some soup. We don't get charged for the water. When we pay the check, the woman at the cash register, in accented English, tells us we're a very *pretty couple*. I think Gretchen likes that. We each take a wintergreen mint out of a bowl as we leave for dessert.

It's dark but it's still pretty early and so we decide to take a walk down on the beach. We walk down the old wooden stairs, dump our shoes and go barefoot. We're above the tide line and the sand is cool, dry, and soft beneath our feet. I have to admit the sound of crashing waves is very romantic. I can tell Gretchen's cold and so I give her Dad's jacket to wear. She doesn't want to take it at first, she's afraid I'll be cold, but I tell her I won't be and I'm not. The jacket is like an overcoat on her.

Somehow or another as we walk, we start holding hands again. We're quiet but it's an okay quiet. We stop. We're sort of hugging one another. Gretchen has one hand on my shoulder and the other on my face. I have my hands underneath the jacket and on her waist. Gretchen doesn't say anything, she just looks at me, the tips of her fingers touching my cheek. I can feel the warmth and color rising. My mark is an erogenous zone, one I never knew I had. I kiss Gretchen's palm. She gasps slightly as the tip of my tongue traces her lifeline.

"Ooh," she whispers.

"Ooh yourself," I say. I'm suddenly feeling very James Bond–like—Daniel Craig, not Pierce Brosnan.

Gretchen giggles. She looks away. She's quiet for a moment. And then she knocks me flat. "Billy? How come you've never tried to . . . you know . . ." She searches for the right words and can't find them. But I know what she's talking about. Other than that night on the Ferris wheel, our physical relationship hasn't gone much beyond wild, crazy-making kisses.

"I don't know," I say, not feeling nearly so James Bondish anymore. "I mean, I really *want* to, I do, but—" It feels awkward to tell her the truth. "I don't know if *you* do."

The wind blows her hair. Strands of it touch my mouth. I can feel Gretchen's belly, hard and flat, against mine. She looks at me. She looks into my eyes. She looks deep into my eyes and she asks me with her eyes to ask and ask again.

48

"Are you a virgin?"

Gretchen whispers the question in my ear. I've put the jacket on the sand underneath her. Her tongue tastes of wintergreen. I have my hand under her dress. I can't believe how soft and wet she is.

"Yes," I say. "Are you?"

"No," she says. "Is that all right?"

"Of course it is," I say. "You're beautiful," I say.

"Touch me here," she says, guiding my hand, and when I do she half murmurs, half moans. After a while her hand goes to my belly and then slides lower.

It goes too fast the first time. All the things I thought I'd do and say go right out the window. I'm too excited and the feel, the very *idea*, of what I'm doing makes me cum the moment I enter her.

"I'm sorry," I say.

"It's a compliment," she says. Which is a really nice to thing to say. It makes me feel better. I stay inside her. I can feel her softly squeezing me. "I didn't know you could do that," I whisper. She just giggles.

It takes much longer the second time and is so much better.

My orgasm begins as a tickle somewhere out on the far side of the moon, so quiet I'm hardly aware of it at first. By the time it hits the earth's atmosphere, I'm both inside and outside myself, praying to it.

"Do you believe in God, Billy?"

Dorie once asked me this from her hospital bed.

"No. Do you?"

"I do. Yes. I can't help it."

"It's cool that you do. I wish I did."

"If God *does* exist," says Dorie, smiling her Dorie smile, "what do you think *she* looks like?"

We laughed.

I could tell her now. I can tell Dorie all about God. If God exists, her face is that of the woman looking up into my own.

". . . reason to believe that this involves young people so if you see anything, hear anything, know anything, it is your responsibility as citizens to inform . . ."

If the policeman who arrested Twom for driving his grandmother's car looked like Arnold Schwarzenegger's nephew, the guy on the stage must be his uncle. He has short hair and a stocky, muscular build. The uniform is tight across his chest and belly. He looks like he wouldn't go down if you hit him with a wood plank.

Cop man.

High School High is being brought up to speed on the Night Visitors and, except for me, Ephraim, Twom, and possibly Deliza, no one in the school auditorium could care less. The Latino kids and the black jocks are numb with boredom, some of them probably so inured to breaking and entering, they might as well be listening to regulations regarding jaywalking. The Asian kids are studying. The surfers are stoned. And even though it's against the rules, practically every other kid in the auditorium has their cell phone in their lap and is tapping away.

No one is listening.

Beatrix has told me that when she was in elementary school, students did bomb drills in case of nuclear attack. They were all herded into school basements, stacked side by side against the wall, and told to duck and cover as if putting your arms over your head was going to ward off a hydrogen bomb. They would then be quickly loaded onto school buses, driven home and dumped off so their parents could drag them into the hastily built, backyard bomb shelter. Kids today wouldn't go into the school basement or a bomb shelter on pain of death because it might cut off their 4G service. And if the bomb ever does drop and the servers go down, my generation, with no phones or iPads, will undoubtedly die of symptoms that resemble drug withdrawal long before they die of radiation poisoning.

". . . when you leave the house, set your alarms."

Twom yawns. Deliza is playing idly with the tips of her hair. Ephraim, however, hangs on the policeman's every word as if it's a death sentence.

"If your family is going out of town, remind your parents to notify their security companies . . ."

"We should confess," Ephraim whispers across Deliza to Twom. His voice is trembling.

"You should go dig a grave in your backyard and bury yourself," Deliza hisses back, not so much as even glancing at him.

"Maybe *you* should." says Ephraim, like a defensive little kid. He turns to me. "Billy?" He says it as if he's hoping I'll agree with him and I find myself almost considering it because, frankly, just like Ephraim, I'm feeling like a small dog trying to shit a large bone.

It's like this.

Everywhere I go lately all I seem to see are patrol cars. I see home security guards on foot checking out gates and fences. I see black-and-whites cruising for no apparent reason. Just this morning on my way to school, I pass some agitated home owner talking with two policemen on his front lawn. He's yelling and gesticulating. The closest I've ever gotten to his house is right here on the sidewalk but still the cop turns and yells at me.

"You with the cheap, crappy coverup on your face! I'm talking to you, Normal Man! Get your ass over here."

Actually he doesn't say that.

But as one of the policemen turns and glances at me, I feel as if he might. The cruiser is parked on the street and I have to go around it. Looking through the open window, I see that there is an ugly but very efficient-looking onboard computer installed in the dash and a nasty-looking riot gun mounted on the metal screen behind the front seat. I flash on Twom sitting in the uncushioned backseat, his hands cuffed in front of him. Only instead of Twom it's me. And unlike Twom, I'm not handling it well at all. The problem is I have something to lose now.

Gretchen.

It absolutely kills me that I've done something so incredibly stupid as to fall madly in love. I keep telling myself it's nothing but infatuation, that sooner or later this whole "I can't wait to see you" period will be over. But there's a big part of me that doesn't want it to be. It's ridiculous. Gretchen and I eat lunch together. We unashamedly meet between classes. I borrow Mom's cell phone so we can call one another at night. I've even gotten an e-mail account—*unferth@gmail.com*—so I can write notes to her.

On the weekend, we'll say we're going to the movies, Gretchen will pick me in the family van and we'll go to the mall, park in the parking garage and screw each other's brains out in the back. Once when her parents and sisters are out, we go over to her house and up to her bedroom. The bed, the sheets, the drapes, the covers, the smell of her everywhere—it's wonderful. Having seen Twom and Deliza do it, I've discovered the joys of oral sex. I can't believe how much I like it, making Gretchen gasp and pull on my hair and murmur my name. And when she takes me into her mouth I immediately turn into a quivering, slack-jawed, semiparalyzed anthropoid.

"Wow, that was *a lot*," Gretchen says, and the way she says it, as if it was the very last thing she expected, makes the two of us laugh until we can hardly breathe. Not in my wildest imagination has it ever occurred to me that sex can be funny. It makes me like it even more.

But it's not just sex.

I find that I enjoy going to watch Gretchen run after school at track practice. I'll sit high in the stands above the track with a book and sometimes I won't even pretend to read. I can't believe how great she looks in her running shorts and shirt, with her red hair pulled back in this long braid that goes down her back. She reminds me of an Amazon huntress.

Point of reference.

In Greek mythology the Amazons were this nation of beautiful women warriors who cut off one of their boobs because it got in the way of shooting their bows and arrows. When they weren't hunting and killing things, their modus operandi—which is Latin for method of operation—was to go around kidnapping men and then screw them totally senseless so as to impregnate themselves. Once the mission was accomplished—*datum perficiemus munus*—they'd cut the guy's throat.

Thankfully, nobody on the girls' track team has cut off a boob and/or killed anyone yet. At least I don't think they have. However, there's no doubt they're all very good at running and you could only wish for the screwed-senseless part.

Gretchen's specialty is the fifteen hundred meters, which is this crazed all-out race that goes three and a half times around the track. It's insane how they train for it. Gretchen and the other girls will be jogging along and all of sudden they'll break into an all-out sprint that lasts about a minute and a half but seems like an endless lifetime. And then, they'll stop and smoothly jog again for a little while. And then, unbelievably, they'll suddenly kick it up into high gear again. You get exhausted just watching them.

When they finish the sprinting, even from a distance, I can see that Gretchen's entire body is flushed pink, which is the way it always is after we've had sex. This makes me wonder if running wouldn't be another fun thing Gretchen and I could do together, and so, at my suggestion, we go to the track one evening and, wearing shorts and sneakers, I run with her. I last for about three laps and, as opposed to fun, all I feel is the urge to fall into the high jump pit, puke and die.

So much for that.

The other thing I really like is when Gretchen has an actual track meet. They save the fifteen hundred meters for toward the end because it's a big deal and I start getting nervous even before Gretchen and the other runners come to the starting line. They stand there, all of them different sizes but all of them in really great shape, and then all of a sudden they're off and running in this closely bunched pack. They're all elbowing and pushing and jockeying for position. They're going stupid fast and you know they haven't even warmed up yet. After a couple of laps it usually comes down to Gretchen and two other girls, and by the time they're into the last lap I'm on my feet, screaming like some idiot, because I want her to win so much. In the last ten yards or so she usually does.

After Gretchen has walked around for a while and caught her breath, she'll look up in the stands for me, and when she sees me she'll give me this huge wave and big smile like she's totally thrilled and it's made her day that I'm there. And I'll be smiling and waving back at her because I'm thrilled too.

That's the best part. This is the worst part.

When I'm doing all this insane stuff, every now and then, I sort of experience what I assume is a feeling of unexpected joy and happiness. The world suddenly seems like it has the potential to be an okay place. And this bothers me because I know deep inside the world isn't and never will be. I know this relationship is not going to last forever, that like with Dorie, like with what's happening to Mom and Dad, it's going to wither and die and I am going to miss it *so much* when it's gone.

Still.

For the time being it's as good a reason as any not to get into trouble.

50

"I asked for the transcripts of your SATs."

This is the Tuesday morning in March when I've been called into the guidance office by Miss Barber. I assume it's going to be about more applying-to-college stuff and it is. Sort of.

"Math is 610, writing 620, critical reading 590," Miss Barber says. "Middle of the pack."

She's holding the printed transcript out to me as if she thinks I want to take it and look at it. I don't. She pulls it back.

"What I find interesting, though," Miss Barber says, turning the page, "is the unscored variable section." She looks at me. "The part that's used to try out new questions for future SATs?"

My stomach sinks. I know where this is going now.

"Almost 800 on a critical reading section," Miss Barber says, "which would put you in the ninety-ninth percentile. On a section that's probably more difficult than the SAT itself."

I'm such an idiot. You're not supposed to know which

is the experimental stuff but it's so obvious. For some stupid reason, I thought it'd be interesting to give it a real go. It never occurred to me anybody was going to grade me on it.

"That's really hard to believe," I say. "Because I was just fooling around."

From the way Miss Barber looks at me, I can tell she doesn't buy it. "What is going on with you, Billy? What's going through that brain of yours? I know you have one."

I don't know what to say to that so I don't say anything.

"I'm going to recommend," says Miss Barber, "that you see a school-appointed psychologist."

51

"Billy's school guidance counselor thinks it would be a good idea for him to see a psychologist," Mom says quietly.

It's a beautiful evening and we're having dinner outdoors on the back patio. It's Dad's favorite, filet mignon, baked potatoes, and a lettuce wedge with Roquefort dressing, but I can tell he's all of a sudden expecting serious indigestion.

"I thought we were over that," he says, dumping a thick wad of butter into his potato.

By "over that," Dad is referring to the fact that a year after Dorie died, I was still feeling sad on occasion and Mom thought it would be a good idea for me to see a psychologist for evaluation. Dad was against it.

"It's four hundred bucks an hour," said Dad.

"We can afford it," said Mom.

"You sure the kid's not just feeling sorry for himself?" said Dad.

"He's not," said Mom.

"Yeah, well, what are people going to think?"

"I don't *care* what they think. I think we *all* should be seeing someone."

"Not some quack of a shrink!" Still a blue-collar laborer at heart, Dad thought the whole idea of therapy was bogus.

And it was.

On the moron scale, Dr. Belafonte, who wasn't even a doctor, just a Ph.D. and who left magazines like *Car and Driver* and *Road and Track* in the waiting room for his whacked-out patients, was a possible twelve. About the only thing he assessed was that I was possibly an apopheniac, which meant I had, depending on your definition, either a talent or a psychosis for formulating meaningful connections out of random data. At that point Dad, who equated weird behavior with his mother, said enough was enough, and despite Mom's protests, that was it for Dr. Belafonte.

Until now.

"We *are* over it," I say. "Really, I'm fine. Really. I'm really fine. Miss Barber's making a big thing out of nothing." Even though I'm not crazy about steak, I take a big bite and chew it to show how healthy my appetite is.

"She says she doesn't think Billy is trying in school," Mom says. "She says he's too smart to be getting the grades he's been getting."

"What? He's not failing," says Dad. He takes a suspicious swallow of wine. "Is he?"

"*No,*" Mom says. You can tell she wants to remind him that there *are* such things as report cards and there *are* parents who occasionally look at them.

"Then what's the big deal?" says Dad. "School's over-rated anyway."

"Gordon, it is *not*. It's important."

"So what's a shrink going to do, take his tests for him?"

Shaking her head, Mom pushes some meat around her plate with a fork. She's not really eating, just cutting her food into smaller and smaller bites. "I can't believe I wasn't paying attention to this. You and your sister always got such wonderful grades."

"Aw, if you're going to start *blaming* yourself again," says Dad, tossing his napkin down on the table.

Mistake. They glare at one another. It suddenly has the potential to get very ugly and so I jump in. "It's no one's fault," I say. "I'm trying. I really am. Really. But it's hard."

Mom turns to me. "The guidance counselor says you haven't even been applying to colleges. Why did you tell us you were?"

Shit. This is true. I even gave them a fake list. "I didn't want you to worry about me," I say. This is also true. Not to mention, I didn't feel like having to talk about it.

"Oh, honey," says Mom, concerned now. Which is the last thing I want.

"But I thought I'd apply to college next year," I say. "When I have a better idea what I really want to do in life."

"I think a job would teach you a thing or two about life," says Dad. You just know he's going to start his "when I was a kid" spiel any second. Mom cuts him off.

"You're not having trouble sleeping again, are you, honey?"

This is the *very* last place I want to go. "No," I say to her. "I'm sleeping well all the time. I really am. Really."

"I don't know," says Mom. "Maybe we *should* see Dr. Belafonte again."

"Oh, for Christ's sake!" says Dad.

"Stop it!" shouts Mom.

Dad should really shut up now if he knows what's good for him. But Dad doesn't know what's good for anybody anymore.

"What? We do it *your* way? Like always? That does a lot!"

Mom's eyes are closed now. She might be softly humming to herself. The look on Dad's face says he knows he's gone way too far but it's too late to go back. Dad never cries but right now it looks like he could.

"I wish you'd let Miss Barber handle it," I finally say. "I really think she knows what she's doing."

It's what we do. It's easy, it takes them off the hook, and it's something they can both agree on without fighting.

Question.

Does loving someone give you permission to be furious with them? Or are you furious with them because you're no longer in love?

52

High School Highville South is a beach community of college students and young families, also old surf vagabonds who spend the mornings sitting in front of Denny's and the afternoons getting stoned or drunk and sleeping on the beach. There are bars and inexpensive restaurants and bike and surf shops and clothing stores. There are a lot of modest houses, condos, and apartment buildings. Miss Barber lives in a nondescript building about a half mile from the ocean. Ephraim has found the address by accessing the school's private directory.

It's a Friday. I'm skipping school.

When the young guy carrying a surfboard comes out of the apartment building and trots across the lawn, I move out from between the two cars where I've been waiting. I get to the security door just before it closes and I grab it. There is a wall of anonymous-looking mailboxes just outside the door, very much like the ones at Mailboxes and More. There's a panel of call buttons. Anne Barber is in 3B. I press the call button. I know Miss Barber isn't in, but I want to make sure no one else is. I ring several times. There's no answer. I go in, shutting the security door behind me.

I take the stairs. I don't want to chance getting stuck with anyone on the elevator. When I get to 3B, I take out the EZ Snap Lock Pick Gun, insert the pick and pull the trigger twice. I open the door and I'm in.

The apartment is nothing special. It's neat. It's clean. You get the feeling Miss Barber hasn't been here long and doesn't plan on staying forever. There is a kitchen to the right as I enter. There is a toaster, a blender, and a Krups coffeemaker on the counter. There's sparkling water and nonfat yogurt in the fridge. There's an adjacent dining area to the left with a sideboard, a small table, and four chairs. On the table are place mats and two inexpensive candlesticks. The candles are burned down. There's an open bottle of red wine—Two-Buck Chuck from Trader Joe's—on the sideboard. Though he probably couldn't tell the difference in a blind tasting, Dad would not approve.

There's an alcove. It's the workspace of a teacher. A small desk. An office chair. A PC. Books and papers. Diplomas on the wall. Miss Barber has graduated from the University of Wisconsin, Madison. She's gotten a graduate degree in education from UC Santa Barbara. There are a couple of sports pennants on the wall. Wisconsin's school mascot is the badger. A badger is a vicious, short-legged weasel. SCSB's mascot is the gaucho. A gaucho is an Argentinean cowboy. An Argentinean cowboy has as much to do with the history of California as a kumquat. I have no idea what weasels have to do with the history of Wisconsin.

The living room has a couch, an apple-crate coffee table, an overstuffed chair and rug. The couch faces a wide-screen TV. There is a Blu-ray player beneath the TV. There are shelves lined with DVDs. Miss Barber is a movie buff. There is an iPod dock that connects to an AV system. The living room opens out onto a tiny deck where Miss Barber keeps a plant and a small barbecue. I pull the curtains.

In the bedroom, the queen-sized mattress is on a metal frame with a curved headboard. The duvet and pillow covers are pale blue. There's a patterned quilt at the foot of the bed.

It beckons to me. When I close my eyes to resist, I grow dizzy. How long has it been since I slept for more than an hour at a time?

I have no idea where to begin. I have no idea what I'm looking for. I decide to look at memories.

Miss Barber doesn't keep actual photographs. The albums I've found and studied in most houses are kept by predigital people brought up on twenty-four-shot film that they had to have developed. Their photos are in frames or albums or falling out of boxes in the closet.

I find Miss Barber's memories on her computer. I run a slide show of Miss Barber, her family and friends. They are in turn casual, festive, formal. The people in the photos are being silly, are smiling, making faces, are pretty, are dressed up, are wet. I up the speed of the slide show. Miss Barber's family reminds me of Gretchen's. Miss Barber has nice-looking parents. The kind they grow in

Wisconsin. She has an older sister and a brother. Miss Barber was a bridesmaid at her sister's wedding. It looks like she might have caught the bouquet. I go to Hawaii with Miss Barber and some girlfriends. Tan, smiling, young women in bathing suits hold fruit drinks. They wear flowered leis around their necks. Miss Barber looks good in a bikini top and a grass skirt. Miss Barber and one of her friends go backpacking in what looks like the Yosemite Valley. Miss Barber goes to a Halloween party dressed as a freckled-face baseball player, eye black across her cheeks, her hat tipped sideways. She and her friends are a team. I check the photos to see if Dad is at the party dressed as Abraham Lincoln.

I'm getting nowhere.

I abandon the PC and go through dresser drawers and closets. Besides the usual jeans and slacks and shoes and shirts and skirts, I find Lycra shorts, sports bras, and any number of pairs of running shoes. On the dresser is a single framed photo of Miss Barber and the Yosemite friend with racing bibs on. They are smiling with exhaustion and are slick with sweat. Miss Barber is a triathlete.

Maybe Gretchen will be, too, someday.

I go through the medicine cabinet. There's not even ibuprofen. I go through the mail. I go through old bills and bank statements. Miss Barber has no debt on her credit card. She has a little over eighteen thousand dollars in her savings.

I go through the DVDs. Miss Barber has eclectic tastes. *Room With a View. Boys Don't Cry. Singing in the Rain. Zero*

Dark Thirty. It's when I find the Disney movies that I stop, abruptly sickened by what I'm doing. *Cinderella*. *Snow White*. *Bambi*. *Robin Hood*. *Aladdin*. *The Little Mermaid*. *Finding Nemo*. *Toy Story*.

All Dorie's favorites.

Dumbo. The little elephant with big ears. The little elephant who flies. Mrs. Jumbo trumpets for her child, only to be imprisoned in a railroad car. Dumbo comes to her in the rain, her trunk snakes out between the prison bars and entwines with his. Dumbo rubs his cheek against it and takes comfort.

This is all on Miss Barber. If it wasn't for her I wouldn't *be* here, wouldn't be doing this, looking for an advantage, trying to find a leg up, just in general a pathetic dick.

I almost hit the ceiling as, like a sudden air raid alert, the phone rings. I stare at it, my heart pounding. It rings again. Another ring. Another. They seem to go on forever. The machine finally takes the call and I hear Miss Barber's voice.

"Hi, this is Annie. You know the drill. Have a great day."

It's a woman's voice. It's trembling.

"Annie, it's Joan. I'd call your cell but . . ."

She hesitates and then it comes out in a sudden rush.

"I'm afraid you'll answer and I'd have to talk and you're not there right now, you're working, and so I . . ."

The woman's voice cracks.

"Annie, I know I told you I was leaving Paul but . . ."

It breaks again.

"I *can't*. I keep trying to tell him. I mean, I think of you and I get to the door . . . but then . . . I keep going *back*."

The photos I merely glanced at now fill my head. Vacations with girlfriends. Women in bathing suits and racing bibs. Baseball player costumes. A friend who isn't just a friend but is now a voice on an answering machine trying not to cry.

The voice moans.

"I'm not strong like you, Annie . . . I want my marriage. I want a baby. I want to be like *other* people."

There are no words for what seems like a long time. Just a human being crying, mumbling, and choking on despair.

". . . please understand. And maybe forgive me," the voice finally says. "But please . . . don't call. I can't talk to you anymore. I love you so much and it's too hard."

The voice hesitates as if the person it belongs to has a noose around her neck and is ready to kick the chair over. And then she does.

"Bye."

The voice hangs up. I cross the room to the answering machine. Its light blinks. Evidence of a call. I can leave now. What could I ever do that hasn't just been done?

I reach out and I erase the message.

The following Wednesday afternoon I pass Miss Barber in the hall between classes. She's been absent since the beginning of the week. Her face is strained. There are shadows under her eyes. She doesn't see me. She doesn't see anyone.

The subject of the school-appointed psychologist doesn't come up again. Miss Barber obviously has a lot on her mind.

53

Three.

Three is the numeric quality of inevitable events. I, you, and we express all the possible relationships of man, while thought, word, and deed define his actions. Jesus and two thieves were crucified together. In the trenches of World War I, the third soldier to light a cigarette from the same match was considered unlucky because a sniper might see the first light, take aim on the second and fire on the third. When drowning swimmers go under for the third time they don't come up. Three strikes you're out.

54

One.

It's a Monday and High School High is letting out for the day. Deliza's Mercedes is parked at the curb. I haven't seen much of Twom lately. I'm spending all my time with Gretchen and he's always with Deliza. But today Deliza has some errand she has to go do with her mother and so Twom and I are planning on hanging out.

Gretchen and I sit on a low wall, saying good-bye. It's taking a long time and is very enjoyable.

Deliza is in the front seat of the Mercedes and Twom is standing in the street, leaning in the driver's-side window. They murmur to one another, they kiss. It would be embarrassing except Gretchen and I are doing the same stupid thing.

I first hear and then, looking up, see the car approach down the hill. I immediately know who it is. Kids on the sidewalk jump back as the Boxster abruptly brakes, swerves in close to the Mercedes, and stops just before hitting Twom. The top is down. John Montebello leans on the horn.

Fact.

Apprehension is the feeling or anticipation that something bad or evil is going to happen.

"Hey! Move it, Willard! The street is for cars, not retards," yells Montebello. There are no cars coming from either direction. He could go around easily but he doesn't. Twom slowly turns to face him. His eyes are like marbles.

"Someone must have had brave pills for breakfast," I hear Twom say.

I see Montebello raise a pint of vodka. He grins, toasts Twom, and takes a quick hit. He glances over toward me. Gretchen is still beside me. I can feel the sudden tension in her.

"Hey, pie face, you tapping that cooze? I sure did."

I quickly look at Gretchen. I see by her shocked expression that Montebello is telling the truth. I'm on my feet in an instant, across the walk, off the curb, and into the open car. I'm swinging wildly. I'm an insane man. Nose cartilage cracks. I break teeth. I draw blood.

"Take it back! Take it back!"

I don't do anything.

I sit there, hardly breathing, feeling hollow inside. Billy Kinsey. The Stained Knight. Too meek to protect the meek.

Twom is not.

I see him turn away from Deliza. I see him leap up onto the hood of the Boxster convertible. He does it like it's easy, does it like he's weightless. He isn't. The hood of the small car buckles under his heavy boots. Twom stares down through the windshield at John Montebello.

Kids are gathering on the sidewalk to watch.

"Say something else," I hear Twom say. "Go on. Anything. I'll stick that bottle down your throat."

Montebello's teeth are clenched, his jaw is trembling. "Try it and I'll sue your ass," says Montebello.

"And I will *kill* you." Twom actually snarls as he says it. "I will come to your house in the middle of the night and I will murder you in your sleep." He says it, and the way he says it, makes everyone—*everyone*—know he will do it and not care about the consequences. Montebello has everything to lose. Twom has nothing.

"Apologize," Twom says.

Montebello looks startled. "What?"

"I said, apologize to her!"

Montebello shakes his head, trying to look amused, trying to act as if Twom is some poor shithead who can't take a joke. He shrugs as if it's no big deal. "Hey!" Montebello calls out. "Gretch, I'm sorry! Just fooling around, y'know?"

Gretchen is staring down at the sidewalk. It's hard to say if she's heard him or not. Deliza answers for her.

"Go fuck a dog, you pale piece of shit."

Someone on the sidewalk laughs. Montebello's head jerks as if he's been slapped. He turns to see who it is.

"Now him," says Twom.

"What?"

"Billy too."

I don't want him to. I pray to God he won't.

"Do it!" shouts Twom.

"Kinsey!" calls John Montebello. "Sorry, dude, I'm just messin' with you. We're buds, right?"

Under the cheap actor's makeup that has fooled me into thinking I'm like other people, the hemangioma feels like a bleeding, black scab.

"Sure," I say.

I really say that.

"I see you again——" says Twom. He doesn't finish the sentence. He hawks, leans forward, and spits on the windshield of Montebello's car.

Someone on the sidewalk laughs again. Others join in. The sound is of hens cackling. Montebello inhales it like smoke.

It happens so fast.

Twom turns on the hood of the car and jumps down. As his feet touch the ground, Montebello pops the clutch and hits the gas. Deliza screams as the front bumper of the car strikes Twom above the knees and sends him sprawling back up onto the hood and headfirst into the windshield. As the car accelerates, Twom rolls off to the side and falls into the street, landing on his head, back, and shoulders. The car stops. Montebello looks back as if stunned at what he's done. Twom isn't moving. Deliza is still screaming as she gets out of the Mercedes. As Montebello drives away, she runs down the street to Twom. She kneels at his side, prodding at him, begging him to get up, wailing.

I can't seem to move. Like all the other students at High School High I just stand and watch.

It takes a teacher to call 911.

55

I was in a hospital waiting room, waiting to go see Dorie when Dad came out, sat down and quietly told me she was dead. It wasn't even the leukemia. Dorie died of sepsis.

Fact.

Sepsis is when your blood is overwhelmed by bacteria and germs and your body breaks down one organ at a time.

Sidebar.

It was the hospital that killed Dorie.

And now it's after school the next day and I'm sitting in the same horrible waiting room with Ephraim. The room is still small, the furniture is still uncomfortable, and the magazines are still torn, tattered, and so out of date, the celebrities on the covers are no longer in the public Zeitgeist. High on the adjacent wall, on a flat-screen TV, ESPN sportscasters are arguing about hockey. No one has the energy to find the remote clicker that will turn it off.

The room still smells of worry and death.

All night long, in text messages, e-mails, and phone

calls, High School Highville has been buzzing with what happened. Truth might be stranger than fiction but it's not nearly so breathless. It was a gang hit involving drugs, sex, and the Mexican mafia, and for her own protection, Deliza Baraza has been taken to a monastery in Monterey by her father. A third of the student body, approximately four hundred people, was actually there and they are all now in the Federal Witness Protection Program. A number of innocent bystanders, including an infant and a janitor, have been taken into custody for questioning. Cell phone footage of Twom lying in the street has been uploaded to YouTube and the ever infatuated Ophelia is organizing a nationwide candlelight vigil for him a week from Thursday.

When your life is shaped and influenced by the unreality that is TV and movies, you make life unreal.

On the *real* front, Gretchen didn't come to school today.

Ephraim sits near me, looking as if someone ran over his pet rabbit. It was Ephraim who showed me the YouTube footage. On his iPhone. Twom, lying in the street, looks dead, and Deliza, crouched over him, looks like a woman whose family was in a mosque and it's just been bombed.

I'm nowhere to be seen.

Ephraim and I both stand up as Twom's grandmother comes into the waiting room. "So it's you two," she says. She looks more annoyed than anything else. It's as if this whole thing is really a terrible imposition that she shouldn't have to be dealing with, not when she could be out shopping for cigarettes, discount gin, and dog food. "Go on in if you want," she says. "He's awake." She's already reaching for her smokes as she hightails it down the hall.

We find Twom in a room with two other patients. One of them is some unconscious old guy, his eyes closed, his mouth open in a slack-jawed O. It's hard to tell whether he's dead or sleeping. The second patient is moaning from behind a drawn curtain.

"Mother, give me your hand . . . !"

Twom is in a bed. He has an air cast on his left wrist. He has tubes in his right forearm. The side of his face looks like it was stuck in a Cuisinart. His eyes are closed.

"Twom?"

When Twom opens his eyes you can see that the sclera, the white part surrounding the iris, is stained with the bright red patches of hemorrhaged blood vessels. Twom tries to smile but fails miserably. "Whassup, dudes?" He lisps slightly because his front teeth are broken. I shrug as if him being in a hospital bed with a concussion and a lacerated spleen is no big deal.

"Not much," I say. "You?"

"Landed on my head, no problem." It's a cool thing to say. Twom falls back against the pillows. He looks exhausted. "Someone please tell me they threw that fucker in jail."

Ephraim and I glance at one another. The news started making the rounds on High School High's frantic information network around one in the afternoon.

"What?" says Twom, seeing our faces. He rises up slightly.

"He's saying it was an accident," I tell him. "That his foot slipped off the clutch. He kept going because he was scared of you."

I might as well smack Twom in the head with a car again. "They believe that?" he says.

"You hit him with a lunch tray," says Ephraim, as if that answers everything.

Twom closes his eyes and settles weakly back against his pillow. He has the look of someone who has been screwed by the system his entire life and the one time he thought he could trust it, it screwed him again and now he knows it always will.

"I'm gonna go in and wipe out his bank account," says Ephraim. Like it's something one of his superheroes would do.

"Yeah. That'll fix him."

Ephraim and I turn to see Deliza standing in the doorway. It's hard to say how long she's been standing there. She looks furious. Hardly glancing at us, she enters and moves to the side of the bed. She takes Twom's uninjured hand in her own.

"Hey, Twomey, I'm here, baby. I'm here," she whispers.

Twom's eyes open. He is crying.

Deliza kisses the tattoos on his hand and wrist. She smiles. "You look like crap, *guapo*."

Guapo. Handsome.

The look they give one another surprises me. It's full

of tenderness and warmth and I realize it's not all just about screwing between them.

Deliza turns to me and Ephraim. She looks angry again. Angry that we're here in the room or maybe just angry at me, angry that I didn't do anything, angry that if I'd been a man, Twom wouldn't be here. Angry maybe because *I* should be the one lying in the bed. "Only two visitors at a time," she says. "One of you has to leave."

Twom doesn't even think to hesitate. "Get out of here, Ephraim."

Ephraim's eyes blink rapidly behind his glasses. He licks his lips, which I now notice are badly chapped. "Why me?" he says.

"Because no one wants you *around*," snaps Deliza.

As Ephraim turns for the door, the expression on his face is that of a little kid, lost on a crowded fairgrounds, not sure where to go or who to ask for help.

"Mother, please give me your *hannnddd...*" moans the guy behind the curtain.

For the first time, I know that it's all going to end so very badly.

56

Two.

I hear the sound of voices.

I'm in the family room, where the family never sits together, staring at the TV which is not on. It's late and I'm tired from the hospital but I don't want to even *try* and sleep. I'm thinking maybe I'll go down to the drum room and bash the crazies out.

If I'm thinking at all.

The voices come from upstairs. They belong to Mom and Dad. *Linda and Gordon.* My parents.

The voices go back and forth, muffled but getting louder and more emotional in pitch. Dad's the kind of guy who has to get mad and yell to express his emotions. Mom is the kind of woman who cries when he yells at her. Which makes him feel guilty. Which infuriates him even more and makes him yell louder. A door opens upstairs. I can hear words now.

"I can't, goddammit—no more! Not anymore!"

"Stop, just—Gordon, will you stop? This is out of no-where!"

"Are you *crazy*? Are you telling me this is *news* to you?"

"That's exactly what I'm saying!"

I know I should stay in my chair. I know it's none of my business. But I can't help it. I have this insane feeling that maybe I can help them. I *want* to.

When I come out of the family room and into the entryway, they're at the top of the stairs. Dad is in Mom's face, towering over her. Veins in his neck are showing. He's practically spitting.

"You had to make this *hard*, didn't you? You couldn't let it be *easy*!" He's carrying a small suitcase.

"You don't talk to me," Mom cries, "you shut me out! I never know what's wrong or what you're even thinking!"

"Bullshit!" says Dad. "Bullshit!"

I wish I could turn away. But I don't. I can't now.

"Since when are you even *interested* in what I think? You play tennis, for chrissake, you get your fucking *nails* done!"

"I had cancer, goddamn you! *Cancer!*"

"Well, you *don't* anymore!" bellows Dad. Quickly turning from her, he starts down the stairs

"Gordon! Gordon, oh, please, don't—" Mom is begging now. I wish she wouldn't. It's worse than the yelling and crying.

At the bottom of the stairs, Dad moves right past me as if he's afraid to look at me. Mom has collapsed into a seated position on the top step and is sobbing. She sounds like a little girl.

Fact.

Human beings are the only creatures that cry tears of emotion. It's thought crying is an unconscious appeal for the protective presence of a parent.

I turn and go after Dad.

I'm halfway across the yard when I see that the Range Rover is already parked at the end of the driveway out in the street. I don't know how long it's been there. Dad opens the rear door of the car and throws his bag in. As the car light comes on, I see that there is someone sitting in the passenger seat.

"Dad!"

Dad stops. He looks back at me now. The look on his face kills me, it really does. It's the look he had when he came to tell me about Dorie. You know he wants to say something that will make it all right but either he doesn't know what to say or he just can't say it. Or maybe he already did.

Just always remember I love you, okay?

He quickly closes the rear door and gets in the driver's side. I'm close enough to see who's in the car now.

I'd read the diary. I should have known.

Mrs. Taylor.

Dad closes the car door. He starts the car.

"Dad! Don't go! *Daddy!*" I actually call him that. What can I be thinking?

The lights inside the car fade to black as Dad puts it in gear. He and Mrs. Taylor turn to shadows. The car accelerates away. I walk out into the street and watch the

Rover go down the hill. It turns at the bottom. And then it's gone.

"Screw'm!"

I turn in shock. Up and across the street Mr. Taylor is standing in his driveway, next to his car, a Lexus sedan.

"Screw'm t' hell!" He takes a step, staggers and almost falls. I realize that he's drunk. "Fug'm *both!*"

I want to kill him. Kill him for his pig-faced stupidity. For his inebriation. For his total cluelessness.

"Fuck *you!*" I scream. "It's *your* fault! You! You never asked! It was in front of your nose and you never asked her about anything!"

Mr. Taylor doesn't answer. He turns unsteadily to his car, opens the car door, half falls in and then closes the door. Somehow he starts the car up. Putting it in reverse, he backs out way too fast. He crosses the road and the rear wheels of the big Lexus slam hard into the curb. Mr. Taylor slams it into drive and peels out, weaving, barely in control. The car disappears up the street and is gone.

When I go back in the house, Mom is still sitting on the stairs, the same place she was when I left. Her face is numb and expressionless. It scares me.

"Mom? Are you okay?"

She looks up as if she's surprised to see I'm there. "Are you?" she says.

"Sure," I say.

"Then I am too."

She takes a deep breath. She has to use the banister to get to her feet. She makes herself smile so I'll know she loves me and that it's all going to be all right, even though it probably never will be again. Taking careful steps, Mom walks slowly down the hall to her bedroom. And then she's gone too.

57

And now—three.

I come running out of the house. I feel like my brain has snapped. I hear unintelligible sounds coming out of my mouth.

In ancient Babylon the penalty for adultery was death by drowning.

The Taylor house is dark. The front door is open. The alarm isn't set. In the living room, the dachshund is lying on the couch, head on its paws. Its terrified eyes follow me as I cross toward the stairs.

Islamic law regarding adultery calls for death by stoning. In ancient Rome, the sentence was banishment.

The Taylors' bedroom is a mess. Clothes, both men's and women's, are everywhere. The bed is unmade.

I move to the bureau. I open the drawer. I throw clothes aside. I pick up the gun. I can't tell if it's loaded. I assume it is.

Someone somewhere has got to pay for their sins tonight.

Driving is harder than I imagine. The pickup truck is heavy and seems to have a mind of its own. Even going slow, giving it short bursts of gas and then gliding, I cross the center line. I swerve back, veering toward the curb, and then I'm up on the sidewalk. Braking, I hit the pedal too hard, lurching and then abruptly stopping. I don't care. I'm no more dangerous than Mr. Taylor. I'm no more dangerous than any drunk driver with a gun on their passenger seat.

I know where I'm going. Even if I hadn't known him since grade school, last August his parents left for a week and he threw an impromptu party. The address was posted on every social network at High School High. I didn't go, but three hundred other people did. They were still talking about the carnage when school started in September.

The Porsche Boxster is parked in the driveway. I pull in as close to the sidewalk as I can. I turn off the truck's engine. I turn off the headlights. I get out. I close the car door as quietly as I can. Lights are on in the house. I cross the lawn and walk around toward the side of the house. The wooden gate is unlocked. It squeaks slightly as I open it. Next door, a dog yaps shrilly. I wait for it to shut up.

In the backyard, double French doors open onto a brick patio. From where I stand, out beyond the edge of the light, I can see John Montebello sitting on a couch, watching television. He looks sullen and bored as if the only exciting thing he's ever done in his entire life is half kill someone a day ago.

Mrs. Montebello appears behind him. She's an attractive woman. She's passed her looks on to her son. I can't quite hear what she says to him and I don't hear what he says back but he scowls. Mrs. Montebello says something again and this time I hear his reply.

"Leave me alone!" says John Montebello. The look on his face makes you wonder if he's ever felt anything for anyone but contempt. Shaking her head, Mrs. Montebello turns and disappears. It must be horrible living in the same house with a person like this, even worse knowing you brought him into the world and raised him.

John Montebello picks up a remote and turns off the TV. He tosses the remote aside and gets up. He scratches his stomach and then his balls. He yawns and turns away. A moment later the lights in the room go off. I move across the patio to the French doors. They're open. The gun feels light in my hand.

Determinism is the idea that every event in the universe is determined by a chain of prior events.

Opening the door, I enter and move across the room as quietly as I can. I enter a hallway. The floors are carpeted. The house is quiet.

Free will is an illusion.

There is a light on at the end of the hall.

No actions are uncaused.

His bedroom door is open. His back is to me. He is taking off his shirt, pulling it over his head. He turns in surprise as I enter.

Everything that happens must happen. Anything that doesn't happen, doesn't because prior events have made it impossible at that moment in time. Fate.

I raise the pistol and, as he lifts his hand in alarm, I

shoot John Montebello in the chest. He falls back against the bed and then to the floor. I look down at him. The contemptuous look is gone.

I raise the pistol and place the muzzle against the side of my head and—

—*quickly lower the pistol from the side of my head with a jerk.*

I'm outside the French doors, still on the patio. John Montebello is somewhere in the house, feeding his face with a snack or brushing his teeth or showering or beating off or going to bed.

I turn and retreat back around the side of the house. I run for the truck. I know where to go now. I'll drive slow. I'll get there. I have to. It's the only hope I have left.

58

For some reason it's a popular question on high school physics tests.

Romeo is standing in the rose garden throwing pebbles up at Juliet's window. He wants the pebbles to hit the window without breaking it. He is standing fourteen feet below her window and fifteen away from the base of the house. How fast are the pebbles moving?

Answer 1. In Shakespeare's *Romeo and Juliet,* no one ever throws pebbles at anything and the dimensions of the courtyard are never mentioned. The question is erroneous.

Answer 2. If Romeo had a cell phone, he wouldn't be standing in the garden in the first place. He'd have called Juliet to meet him at the front gate. Because everyone in the entire world now has a cell phone, no one will ever throw pebbles at anyone else's window ever again. The question is irrelevant.

Answer 3. Unlike the rest of the world, I still do not have a cell phone. Therefore I am throwing pebbles at a window.

At 22.11 feet per second.

Inside, a light goes on. A curtain is pulled back. I can see a face looking down at me. The window opens and Gretchen leans out. She looks down at me. Juliet was never such a welcome sight.

She comes out of the house. She's wearing gym shorts and a T-shirt. She looks for me.

"Billy?"

"Here," I say.

I'm standing in the bushes. Even though it's not cold, I'm shivering. She moves toward me and I know she's going to hug me.

"No," I say. "Don't. I'll lose it."

She does anyway. And it's all too much and as hard as I try not to I start half blubbering into her neck.

"I'm so sorry," Gretchen says. "I'm so sorry. It just happened."

"It's all right," I say. "It's all right. It doesn't matter."

"It does! I was so stupid! We were just back and our parents are friends and he asked me out. And he was such a shit after!"

"I should have done something," I say. "I should have hit him! But I was afraid."

"No," Gretchen says. She kisses the blotchy flesh of my cheek. "No! I don't care! I'm glad you didn't."

She kisses my mouth. "Just don't let this do anything to us!" She kisses my cheek again. My mouth again. She kisses my nose. My eyes. It's like a salve. Where her lips touch, the pain goes away.

"I miss Dorie," I say.

Gretchen wordlessly takes me by the hand and leads me into the darkened house.

Fact.

The one thing that can influence fate and all its myriad chain of events is a creative act of the soul.

We don't make love at first.

We're on the first floor, in a small guest room. Gretchen quietly pulls back the bedcover and we get in with our clothes on. We just hold one another. She doesn't ask any questions. She hardly says a word.

"It's like I'm falling," I whisper. "Falling down this deep, deep hole. The bottom is rushing up. Impact just doesn't get any closer."

"So sad," is all she says. "Such a sad, sad boy."

When she feels me starting to get hard, she slips off her gym shorts. I push down my jeans. She rolls over on top of me. She guides me into her. She puts her head down on my shoulder. We lie like that. Not even moving.

"Do you love me, Billy?"

"Yes," I say. "So much. Do you love me?"

She kisses me on the mouth. "I love you with all my heart, Billy Kinsey."

Truth.

We love in order to know we're not alone.

59

When we come out of the guest room, Dr. Quinn is sitting in the kitchen. In a quiet voice, he tells Gretchen to go upstairs to her room. In the same quiet voice he asks me to leave and I do.

60

Easter. Old English translation—eastre—Goddess of the Dawn. Deity of Resurrection and the Returning Light.

In Madrid, a flash mob of one hundred fifty young people celebrate the day by looting a 7-Eleven Store.

So much for bunny rabbits.

In Brazil, a disgruntled mob protesting the Olympics throw three teenage boys off a six-story roof, killing one. In retaliation, soldiers open fire on a crowd of several hundred, most of whom are engaged in Easter mass. Fifty are killed, scores wounded.

So much for jelly beans.

In Nigeria, Islamist terrorists storm a Christian school, killing a teacher and twenty students, while in Eastern Jerusalem, a car bomb kills seventeen Orthodox Jews, including four children. This is just days after a similar blast kills nine Coptic Christians which is just days after an identical blast kills twenty-three Sunni Muslims which is just days after an even bigger blast kills eleven Buddhist monks visiting from Cambodia. Meanwhile in Sumatra, angry tigers trap six poachers in a bamboo tree for the holiday weekend, causing them to miss dinner. Sadly, *these* men are rescued. And as they are, perhaps coincidentally, perhaps not, in the Netherlands medical experts report that due to the frenzied pace with which mankind is destroying wild habitats and disrupting ecosystems, the next deadly pandemic will be a virus that spills from wildlife into human beings. Because of urban density and human interconnectedness, it will kill millions if not billions.

Just another thing to look forward to.

Meanwhile, home on the ranch.

It was the writer Mark Twain who wrote that one of life's most overvalued pleasures is sexual intercourse and one of life's least appreciated pleasures is taking a shit. In popular online videos celebrating the modern rites of spring, young people do both.

In public.

Vegas, Daytona Beach, Panama City, and Cancún. Tour companies offer vacation packages, everything included except the booze, drugs, and condoms. Unfortunately, sallow-faced grunions from the Pacific Northwest, without the money to do anything else, often descend on the shores of High School Highville and take over, bringing their booze, drugs, and condoms with them.

So much for Easter eggs.

It's low tide and Twom and I walk the edge of the surf, staying as far away as possible from the drunken college morons farther up on the beach. Guys wearing board shorts so low their pubic hair is showing keep calling for tramp-stamped girls in Brazilian-cut bikinis to flash their tits. A sound system is blaring. There's the smell of pot in the air.

Twom doesn't look good. The scabs are gone but his face is tired and drawn and not quite his own. Twom's grandmother paid for new front teeth but they don't look right in Twom's mouth. Too white, too straight, too perfect. There's still blood in the corner of one eye. The doctors aren't sure if it will ever go away.

"Montebello's out of town for a week," says Twom. "The whole family. Hawaii."

"So?" I say.

"So I say we go in and trash the place."

This totally stops me in my tracks. "I didn't hear you say that," I say.

"You want I should say it again?" says Twom.

"Last time was the last time," I say.

"Which is what you said last time. Ephraim's in. Dee is in. That leaves you."

"I don't need this," I say, and I turn to walk away. Twom circles and steps in front of me. I try to move around him. He doesn't let me.

"You sleeping much, Billy?"

I can see my reflection in Twom's eyes. Or maybe it's just that I think I can. My face is even more pale and exhausted than his. I don't think I've so much as dozed in two weeks. Twom knows this. He knows why.

.   .   .

"My mom and dad want us to stop for a while."

We're in Gretchen's front yard. She's called and asked me to come over and now she's come out to talk to me. From the tone of her voice on the phone, I know something is up. But I'm not expecting this.

"Are you going listen to them?" My stomach is doing flip-flops. This isn't supposed to happen. I'm the one who's supposed to do the breaking up with her.

"I don't want to . . . but . . ." Gretchen can't seem to look at me. "They're saying I really let them down."

"Why? Because you were screwing your boyfriend in the maid's room?"

Actually I'm not capable of talking.

"It was horrible, Billy. They even made me get an STD test. All these things I never even heard of."

"Thanks, Dad," I say.

I'm trying to be funny but it isn't. It makes it worse. All I can think of is a doctor sticking his fingers in Gretchen's vagina. I realize I'm angry with her. Angry that she's not braver than this and that she's not standing up for us. I expected more from her, I really did. It's as if she reads my mind.

"They're my *parents*, Billy."

Like it's an excuse. I want to tell her that our parents do everything to us. Yes, they might try to provide for you, and do it because they even care about you and think they have your best interests at heart. But by doing so, they trap you, pure and simple. Even with the best of intentions they can mess you up completely. But I don't say that. I don't say anything at all. I'm dying inside.

Gretchen starts to cry. I hug her. She feels wonderful. I savor everything about her, trying to memorize it.

"Hey. It's a not a problem," I whisper. "I'll wait."

"You will?" Gretchen says. "Promise?"

"As long as it takes," I say. But I won't. I know I won't. I never want to feel like this again. It's just that for this brief and final moment, saying it gives us both a little hope.

Sometimes you don't need a seashell to hear the ocean roaring in your ears.

"Do it for me," says Twom.

He steps back. He stands down. "One more time, that's all. Because if you don't, I *am* gonna have to kill him."

I don't have to ask him who he's talking about. And all of a sudden I realize I want to. Go truly, totally outlaw. I hold out my open palm. Twom taps it with the closed fist of chaos.

Fact.

Revenge is the dark side of justice. He who seeks vengeance digs two graves. One for his enemy. One for himself.

61

"Why, Ephraim, is that you?"

"Hey, Mrs. Kinsey," says Ephraim.

"Well, what a surprise." And not necessarily a nice one.

It's the day after the beach day and we're at my house. Mom glances at me, wondering what this is all about. Mom probably hasn't so much as thought of Ephraim since he was thirteen years old and was caught trying to sell downloaded porno stills from a makeshift stand in front of his house. Ephraim's mother screamed so loud the whole block thought she was killing him. She promptly sent him to off to overnight nerd camp for the rest of the summer.

"How is everything?" says Ephraim. He's trying to be nice. He knows. Everybody in the neighborhood knows.

"Fine, thank you," says Mom. It's anything but. Dad and Mrs. Taylor are living who knows where, Mr. Taylor hasn't returned home, and lawyers are talking. It's already understood that Mom will keep the house. Dad just wants the wine cellar. Mrs. Taylor wants the dachshund.

"We're just going to hang out for a while," I say.

"Have fun." She quickly turns and leaves.

Here's the thing.

I don't think Mom was so much in love with Dad as she isn't sure what she's going to do without him. Even though they were like cars cruising in separate lanes, after almost twenty-something years together, I think she was sort of used to him. And they went through Dorie together.

Here's the second thing.

Both Mom and Dad would have been so much happier not having a lot of money. They weren't ready for it. They weren't trained for it. It wasn't in their DNA. Comfortable would have been just fine. Struggling slightly might have been even better. They would have stayed in Tulare and gone to small-town Fourth of July parades and backyard barbecues. Dad would play golf and go bowling with carpenters and plumbers on weekends. Mom might have taken a part-time job. Summers they would have driven to Yosemite with Dorie and me in a rented RV and we all would have really enjoyed it. When Dorie got sick, Mom and Dad would have felt supported by real friends and neighbors.

Rich people are totally isolated. They live in this state of terror that everything's going to be taken away from them at a moment's notice. You wonder how many of them would just once like a hot dog as opposed to a lobster tail.

I want to tell Mom that she's still pretty nice looking

for someone in her early forties and that she still is rich. One day soon, the house will be filled with suitors feasting on the livestock. I just hope she chooses someone who isn't so desperate and miserable he can't make her happy. In the meantime, she sits around the house, staring into space and sighing. So do I for that matter. Thankfully, Mom's been too preoccupied to notice and worry about me.

"Got it!"

We're in my room. Ephraim is at my desk, on my computer. He's here because his grades have gone to hell, he's failing right and left, and his parents think it will help if they take away all of his computer privileges. This has been like trying to take heroin away from an addict and so of course Ephraim has found other sources. For the first time ever, he's been going to the school library where he can log on. After school, he goes to Kinko's and rents time at a workstation. And at night, under the sheets, he browses the Web with his iPhone which, because of its small keyboard, he doesn't like so much. Now he's on my Mac and even though Ephraim's a PC man it's taken him about two seconds to break into the Montebellos' home security system.

"Write it down," I say.

There's no paper on the desk, and before I can stop him, Ephraim opens the middle drawer, looking for some. He is suddenly very still. The room, the whole house, seems very quiet. Ephraim takes Mr. Taylor's Glock out of the drawer.

"Is this real?"

"Put it back," I say.

Ephraim turns and aims the gun at the wall. Comfortable with it. Ephraim cut his teeth on Doom, if not the first, certainly the graphic best, of all first shooter video games.

"It is, isn't it."

"Put it back, you fuckwad."

"Is it loaded?"

My voice rises. "Now!"

"Okay!"

He puts it back. Reluctantly.

"Now shut the drawer."

He does.

"Now wipe the hard drive."

After he does that, I tell him to go home. After he leaves, I go down to the drum room, take off my clothes, and play until my nails, feet, ears, gums, and nose bleed.

62

A police car cruises the street. It passes the Montebello house. As it turns at the end of the block, we jump out of Deliza's Mercedes, where we've been lying on the seats, and we race across the street. There is the bloodlike taste of copper in my mouth and the fast thump of double bass drums in my chest. I can't seem to take a deep breath. The air is vibrating.

Point of reference.

Oneirophrenia is a hallucinatory state caused by prolonged sleep deprivation. You're not aware of time. You're not attentive to place. The condition makes it impossible to formulate a suitable response to an emotional event.

Translation?

If I don't fall over the edge and down the hill into complete psychosis I should have a wonderful time tonight.

I retrace my steps around the side of the house and the others follow. In the back, I use the EZ pick to open the French doors. We enter to the beeping of the security system. I move to the panel on the wall to key in the code.

I stop.

"What are you doing? C'mon," says Twom. "The code."

I just stand there.

"What the hell, Billy?" says Twom. He sounds tense and annoyed. Maybe he's been experiencing what I felt at Casa de Esperanza. Good.

"Will you just do it!"

I don't.

At that moment the alarm goes off. If it's designed to scare the shit out of any would-be robber, it certainly works. I quickly punch in the code and the alarm goes quiet. Before the phone can ring, I take it off the hook.

"Maybe they'll be here, maybe they won't," I say. "You probably have ten minutes."

"Asshole," says Twom. He and Deliza turn away and are gone.

"What do we *do*?" Ephraim says. He's ready to shred his skin. He has no real idea why he's here.

"I don't care what you do, Ephraim. Just leave me alone."

He hesitates, looking like he wants to implode, and then he runs from the room.

There's nothing I want to do in this house. Explore in this house. Learn in this house. There is no place I will lie down in this house.

I follow my fellow Night Visitors toward the kitchen.

As Deliza rakes shrieking appliances from the countertops, Twom pulls a drawer from a counter and throws it into a glass-fronted cabinet. Crystal glasses disintegrate into dust and broken glass. As he goes for another drawer, Ephraim has the refrigerator open and is sweeping food and jars and bottles out and onto the floor. Deliza picks up a bottle of ketchup and throws it. It explodes on the wall like a blood bomb.

We move into the adjacent family room. Twom and Deliza bring kitchen knives. I watch as artwork is slashed and wallpaper is slit. I do nothing as chairs and sofa are stabbed, cut, and hacked. Stuffing flies like guts and entrails.

I turn as something crashes. Ephraim has pulled a huge, flat-screen TV out of a pewter-colored media cabinet. Wires and cords and veins and arteries tear free and tangle. DVDs fly and fall. Ephraim begins to crazily jump up and down on the television, the look on his face saying he's been wanting to destroy things his entire life and only now does he have the courage and the opportunity to do so.

I move into the dining room just in time to see Twom and Deliza pull a large gilt-framed mirror from the wall.

Breaking a mirror is not just the destruction of your appearance but also the shattering of your soul.

The mirror lands on the dining room chairs and table. It shatters. Shards soar across the room. The floor is covered with scattered reflections. In each one, Deliza laughs like a delighted goblin at a children's party.

There is a gold chandelier above the table. Jumping up onto a chair, Twom grabs it and swings. His weight rips it creaking from the ceiling and it crashes down onto the table, splintering it. The sound reverberates through the entire house.

I turn away. I walk down a hall. I've become like Twom. None of this is really happening and if it is I couldn't care less.

I stop in the doorway to a study just in time see Ephraim pick up a laptop computer—his totem, his brother and sister, his kin. He raises it high and smashes it down on the floor. He picks it up and throws it down again, disengaging battery from deck, life force from carcass.

I turn away.

I follow Twom and Deliza to the garage. I stand watching as Deliza rakes the hood of Montebello's Porsche with a screwdriver. Taking a can of white house paint from a shelf, Twom dumps it onto the seats. It's old and curdled, the color of decaying teeth.

I turn away.

I find Ephraim in a bedroom. He's breaking children's toys one after another. Snatching a stuffed unicorn from the bed, Ephraim rips it to shreds. He turns to see me watching him.

"Get away from me!"

He picks up a book and throws it at me. It bounces off the doorjamb. I look down at it. *Where the Wild Things Are.* The story of a boy who wreaks havoc and runs off to an island inhabited by mythical, fanged beasts. No. The beasts, the wolves—the wild things—are here in this house tonight.

I turn away.

In the master bedroom, Twom pulls drawers out of a bureau and throws them to the floor. He picks up a jew-

THE TRAGIC AGE   **263**

elry box and heaves it at a lamp across the room. Somewhere, somehow he's cut his hands. Laughing, Deliza takes them and, lifting them to her mouth, licks the blood from his knuckles. They kiss feverishly. Twom paws Deliza's breasts with bloody hands. She wraps a leg around Twom's hips, pushing her pelvis against him.

"Stop it!" Ephraim screams from the doorway. "Don't do that!" His eyes are bulging, ready to burst behind his glasses.

Deliza turns her head to look at him. She laughs. Taking a step back, she falls back onto the bed, pulling Twom down on top of her and between her legs.

Ephraim runs.

I watch, not really seeing, as Twom and Deliza begin to have sex on the bed. I'm no longer embarrassed. It's not like it's even them. Whenever I close my eyes, then open them, it's someone else. It's Linda and Gordon. Dad and Mrs. Taylor. Miss Barber and Gretchen. Everyone trying to escape into one another, even if it's just for a moment.

I turn away.

I'm on my way out the back door when I smell the smoke.

63

In the living room, the gas jets of the fireplace are on high. The hissing flames rise from the gas line and fill the entire hearth, blue at the bottom, white at the top. Throw pillows burn in the grate, the down stuffing charring black. Torn, pulled down, silk curtains hang from the mantel in flames. Fire has begun to crawl across the adjacent wall.

Ephraim's back is to me. He is spraying something from an aerosol can onto the wall in grand sweeps. The wallpaper bursts into flames so suddenly that Ephraim throws up an arm to protect himself. He turns, facing me. He is holding the can in one hand. He is holding the gun in the other.

This is not how it happens.

"I told your mother I left my jacket in your room," says Ephraim, brandishing the gun. His voice comes from a sinkhole. His face is stained with soot. His eyes are liquid behind his glasses. Something inside the wall snaps as the heat hits it. Paint bubbles and burns as the fire climbs to-

ward the ceiling where the smoke alarm hangs, discon-
nected and useless.

"I turned it off," says Ephraim. "I turned everything off."

This cannot be how it happens.

"This is so bad, Ephraim. This is so, so bad." It was
from the beginning. We knew it would be. But not this.
"We've got to get out of here."

Ephraim raises the gun and aims it at me. I quickly
back up, wondering if I'll hear it or feel it first.

"You think you're smart. Always so smart? Well, I'm
smart too, you know! I matter too!" Spittle flies from
Ephraim's lips.

"No one ever said you didn't," I say. But no one ever
said you did, I think.

"Fuck that! Fuck it!" Ephraim throws the aerosol can
at me. He misses by a mile. "Ephraim the nerd! Ephraim
the geek! Knock faggot Ephraim down in the shower!"

He's crying. His hopelessness is more frightening
than his anger. He sags. The gun lowers just a bit.

"It's always her, Billy. Why her? Why not me?"

"I don't know what you're talking about."

Ephraim pushes the gun toward my face, furious again.
"Don't say that! Don't say that! You know. You know!"

I do.

"Ephraim, you're my friend," I say. What else is there
to say?

"Am I, Billy? Am I really?" His voice is sad and plain-
tive. He wants to be.

"Sure you are," I say. I try to smile as if it's all okay. "Now c'mon, let's get out of here. We'll go home, order up a pizza, some sodas, it'll all be fine." I sound incredibly reasonable. Considering the circumstances, I'm proud of myself. Maybe I have a future in this. Deal making. Hostage negotiations.

"Yes. Go," says Ephraim, and putting the barrel of the Glock into his mouth, he pulls the trigger.

This is how it happens.

I've turned away. My eyes are closed and I stumble into something—a chair, a couch, furniture. The shot has my ears ringing so loudly I can barely hear myself howl. I tell myself over and over again this is impossible, that it's all part of another bad dream and it's time to wake up now, it's time to wake up. But I know I'm already awake.

I turn back. Ephraim's body is on the floor. He's on his back. His glasses are broken. There is blood in his nose and mouth. His eyes are open and staring. Part of his skull is gone.

It's so easy.

"Billy! Dude! Where are you? Billy?"

I hear voices calling from somewhere else in the house. Maybe the people who own them will keep going. Maybe they'll just leave. They don't.

The two of them enter the room, Twom raises his arm, as if trying to ward off the heat. The synthetic chemical smell of the burning couch stuffing suggests poison.

"What the hell, man!" he says. "What the hell!"

His eyes go from the burning walls to the floor. To Ephraim. To the gun on the floor.

"Oh, Jesus . . ." Twom looks at me. "Billy . . . ?" His look asks the question. *Did you do this?*

"He did it himself," I say. I wonder if I should tell him why. I don't.

Twom moves closer, bends down to view the ruin that is Ephraim's head. He turns away, gagging. "Oh, Jesus, dude. Oh, shit."

"What a *chingado* douche bag," says Deliza. She shakes her head, both furious and disgusted.

I can't believe it.

"What?" I say.

"He was an asshole!" Deliza spits the words at me. "He couldn't do this at home?"

I'm screaming at her before I even know I'm screaming.

"Shut up! Just you shut up! You treated him like crap!" I should stop but I can't stop. I don't want to stop. Fists clenched, I start toward her. "Why don't you get naked in front of his corpse, you bitch!"

Twom quickly steps between us and pushes me back so hard, I stumble and fall. "Both of you just calm the fuck down!"

"It's all going to be just fine," whispers Ephraim's corpse.

Twom picks the gun up off the floor. "We're outta here," he says. "Are you coming?"

I don't move.

"Get out of here, Billy," says Ephraim's body.

I don't move.

"Baby, we gotta go," says Deliza.

Twom hesitates. He shrugs. "Can't wait for you, bro." They turn and hurry from the burning room.

I kneel beside Ephraim. I look down into his broken face. The world will keep turning. He was born too late, that's all. Even his parents will find it easy to let him go. They can travel now.

"Ephraim," I say. "You were my friend." Rising, I follow the only two that remain to me out of the house.

64

There are neighbors in the street but they back away when they see the gun in Twom's hand. Turning to look back, I can see flames through the living room window. Somewhere in the distance I can hear the sound of a siren.

Twom and Deliza leap into the car, Twom hesitating just long enough to aim the gun at a man behind the Mercedes.

"Away from the car!"

The man quickly steps back.

"Billy! Let's go!" I run down the walk and across the street. I clamber into the backseat. Twom puts the gas pedal to the floor, the tires squeal and we're away. When I look back, I see the man is writing something down.

"They have the license plate."

"*Mierda!*" says Deliza. "My father is *so* going to ground me." I actually laugh. Being forced to stay home for the next three months or so without visitors sounds great just now.

"Come on, Billy, you're the brains, what do we do?" I

can see Twom's face in the rearview mirror. It's the first time I've ever seen him in a panic.

"I'll tell you what we do," says Deliza. "We're going to Mexico. We can be across the border into TJ in forty-five minutes. My family has people there."

TJ. Tijuana. Mexico. As in come for our beaches, stay for our kidnappings and decapitations. Of course Deliza would have people there.

"Billy? Come on, what do you think? Say something!"

"Who cares what he thinks!" shouts Deliza.

She's right. *I* don't even care what I think anymore "I need to stop first," I say.

They argue with me for a while but there's no voting on this. It's what we do.

65

I use the EZ pick to open the lock. It hardly takes a moment. I'm good at it now. I key in the security code. I had Ephraim get it for me months ago. I didn't know why. I just wanted it. Maybe I was preparing for a night like this.

I could sleep in this house. Even on the hardwood floor, I could curl up and sleep.

Instead I stand and listen to the sound of Gretchen's breath. Her hair is spread against the white of her pillow. She is on her side. I see the curve of her hip against the blanket. Her room smells faintly of the perfume she wore on Valentine's Day. It makes me aware that my hair and clothes stink of smoke and sweat.

The grandfather clock out in the hallway click-tocks, suddenly rumbles and then chimes once, twice, all the way to eleven times. It's loud and yet I've never been aware of it when in the house before. The clicks and chimes of the clock rumble and then repeat and this time they feel like they're proclaiming the hours of my life, passing, never to be reclaimed.

The art of clock repair is dying. It, too, will never be reclaimed.

The sound of Gretchen's breath changes slightly. She stirs and then suddenly, as if sensing something, she sits up in bed. Holding the sheet and blanket to her chin, she peers into the darkness.

I don't want to scare her.

"Hey. It's just me," I whisper.

"Billy?"

"Yeah. Surprise." Trying to smile, trying to show her that nothing's wrong, I step closer toward the bed. Gretchen doesn't look alarmed as much as puzzled. "How did you get in?"

"I broke in," I say. I show her the EZ pick. It's still in my hand.

"I don't understand," Gretchen says.

"All the break-ins," I say. "The Night Visitors. It's me."

If she's shocked, she doesn't show it. Maybe it's not such a big deal, maybe if I can explain, she'll understand.

"We didn't mean anything. Really. We were just hanging out. And then it got out of hand. It was stupid. I'm sorry we ever did it. I wanted you to know that. How sorry I am."

Outside, on the street, a car horn blares.

"Who's that?" asks Gretchen.

"My ride," I say, trying to make it a joke. The horn sounds again, then a second time, then the third time. How, the horn asks, can the soul create and influence anything if the soul is confused or even empty?

"Listen, I've got to go," I say. "I just wanted to say good-bye, that's all."

"But—where are you going?"

Gretchen throws back the covers and swings her feet to the floor, rising. Her thin nightgown is sleeveless and barely mid-thigh. It seems impossible that I could think of sex at this moment but I do. Maybe it's impossible that I couldn't.

"You can't just leave," says Gretchen.

"Yeah, I can. I want to," I say. I back away. If I look at her another moment, I'll turn to a pillar of salt.

"You said you'd wait."

"You don't understand," I say. I have to swallow so my voice won't break. "Ephraim's dead."

"Who?" She looks confused, as if she doesn't understand.

"Ephraim," I say, insisting. And then it hits me. "You don't even know who he is."

Oh, Ephraim.

The horn blares again.

"I have to go."

We turn as the door swings abruptly open and the overhead lights come on. Dr. Quinn is wearing jeans and a T-shirt.

"What's going on here?"

Gretchen quickly moves between us. "It's okay, Daddy, really, it's okay."

But it's not okay. We all know it's not.

"Gretchen, we asked you not to see this boy anymore.

What is he doing here?" Dr. Quinn sounds quietly furious. Who can blame him?

"I know," Gretchen says. "Please, Daddy, we're just talking."

"Talking? This is your bedroom, Gretchen. You're in your nightgown!"

I step forward, pulling Dr. Quinn's attention to me. "Don't blame her," I say. "Blame me. I broke in and came up to her room." I toss the EZ pick onto the bed. "And now I'm leaving."

As his eyes go to the EZ pick, I brush past him. As I go out the door, I hear Gretchen's voice behind me.

"Daddy, he's running away."

The next thing I know, Dr. Quinn is in the upstairs hallway and following me. Gretchen is behind him. Up ahead, beyond the landing at the top of the stairs, Mrs. Quinn has come out of her bedroom and is pulling on a robe.

"Go back to bed," I say to her. "Please! Just go back to bed!" I'm pleading. I'm begging like Mom did with Gordon. Thinking you love people makes you out of your mind.

"Billy," says Dr. Quinn, on my heels now. "Billy, wait. I apologize. Let's sit down, we'll talk about it. We'll call your folks if you'd like. This isn't the answer to anything, son." He doesn't sound angry anymore, he sounds reasonable. Which makes him more dangerous than ever.

"Jim, shall I call the police?" calls Mrs. Quinn. Her voice is flat and quiet. She is a hospital administrator, just as practical and calm in the face of calamity as her doctor husband.

"No!" Gretchen screams back at her mother. "Go to bed!"

"It's all right, Kath," says Dr. Quinn. And then he's on my heels again. "Billy, I'm asking you to stop. Please, son, this is serious. You're going to stop or I'll have to make you stop."

We're at the top of the stairs, on the landing, when he reaches for me.

"Come on, son."

It happens so fast.

His hand grabs my shoulder. I spin, hitting at it, wanting it off me, wanting to tell him I'm not his son, that I'm no one's son or brother anymore, that there's nothing but a monster in his house. Grendel, the personification of evil, a wild thing, is in his house.

"Please!" I say again.

It doesn't work. Dr. Quinn grabs me with his other hand, holding me, trying to keep me still, and I'm twisting and struggling with him, trying to get away but not able to because he's so much stronger than I am. I'm aware of the sound of frightened little-girl voices and I know it's the twins. I want to tell them I'm sorry but there's no time and I can't talk. Grabbing the banister, I pull away. It's then that my foot slips off the top stair and I start to stumble backward. Dr. Quinn grabs for me, doesn't let me fall, but we're both off balance. As I try to pull away again, his weight goes the wrong way and he staggers.

It doesn't happen like this. Just as with Ephraim, it could never really happen like this.

Dr. Quinn and I, arms around each other, tumble down the stairs together. Dr. Quinn has turned into the fall so that I land on top of him. I can feel him trying to keep me there, using his body to protect me. I hear him grunt as his head strikes one of the hardwood balusters.

Point of fact.

A golf ball hitting a steel plate at 150 miles per hour is filmed at seventy thousand frames per second. In playback, it flattens, spreads like batter on a hot griddle, and then starts to rebound. A nose grows. The nose becomes a lopsided egg. Leaving the griddle, the egg inverts into a lozenge. The lozenge swells into a pear. The golf ball will never be more than a semblance of round again.

Dr. Quinn and I slide to a halt at the bottom step. I'm still half on top of him. He doesn't move.

"I didn't mean to," I say to no one. "I didn't."

Grendel, working evil in the world, did.

"Daddy!"

I look up to see Gretchen racing down the stairs. As I roll off Dr. Quinn, she gets to us and kneels. "Daddy!" she says again.

On the landing, Mrs. Quinn is holding the girls tight to her body. The girls clutch at her robe and are crying.

"Daddy, please," says Gretchen, hands hovering over him.

"Gretchen, don't touch him," yells Mrs. Quinn. She pushes the little girls aside and starts down to us. "Call 911!"

Outside the car horn is keening nonstop. Or maybe

it's my brain. I get to my feet. "I'm sorry," I say. "I'm so sorry." No one is listening.

I run.

When I get outside, Twom shouts something hoarse, garbled, and unintelligible from the open window of the Mercedes. As I come across the front lawn and toward the driveway, I stumble and fall. Twom screams out the car window again. This time he repeats himself so I understand him.

"Come on! Come on, come on, come on, come on!"

It is not encouragement talking, it's desperation.

Or something along those lines.

"You go ahead," calls the oneirophrenia that's filling my head with mad cow disease. "I'm gonna just lie here and beg for mercy."

Unfortunately I don't say that.

Getting to my feet, I hobble toward the car. Somehow I open the rear door and get in. The car is already moving. As Twom backs out of the driveway, I look back at the Quinn house. Lights are on inside. For a moment, I think I see Gretchen on the front porch.

The car turns onto the street, and as it does, I lose sight of everything meaningful. I don't have to look into the rearview mirror to know that the port-wine hemangioma, the badge of my emotions, is now a dark mask that covers my entire face.

66

It happens like this.

Our cab comes east across Camino de la Plaza, passing the Las Americas Premium Outlet Center; over one hundred stores so popular they provide bus tours for shoppers on both sides of the border. The parking lots, sidewalks, and streets are still and deserted, and beyond the stores, looking south over the razor-wire fence that defines the border, you can see the light-dotted hills of nighttime Tijuana.

It was so easy.

Taking our time and never going faster than surrounding traffic, we proceeded south on Interstate 5. Traffic was light. We drove through downtown San Diego without incident. In National City we saw a patrol car pulled over to the side. The policeman was looking out for a motorist as he changed a tire. He didn't glance up at us as we passed. Getting off the highway in Imperial Beach, we dumped the car in a hotel parking lot near the Naval Air Field. The cabs were waiting in front. In Spanish, Deliza told the driver where to go and how she wanted him to get there. The driver shrugged as if to say, it's your money. We continued south avoiding the highway, Twom and I in the back, Deliza in the front, occasionally giving instructions, the driver shrugging and turning.

Now, continuing east toward San Ysidro, we cross the interstate. Below us is the border crossing. On the east side of the bridge, our cab pulls to a stop at the corner of San Ysidro Boulevard. The street is empty. We get out. Deliza pays the driver. She has called her people. They are waiting for us. They are happy to welcome us to their country.

The three of us turn and, hand in hand, begin the short but long walk toward the beginning of a new life.

Never regret anything. At some point you wanted it.

67

The first police car picks us up just north of the San Diego City limits, possibly because the Mercedes has been reported, but more likely because we're doing over a hundred and twenty miles an hour. It comes onto the Interstate 5 about a quarter of a mile behind us, its siren shrieking, the lights on the roof flashing.

It's amazing we've made it this far.

In his mad dash to the freeway, Twom has been driving like a lunatic. We've come down out of the High School Highville on narrow, winding, residential streets going so fast that more than once I've thought we were going to end up in someone's living room. On the flats, the boulevard widens and Twom goes faster still. He switches lanes, passes cars.

"Are you trying to kill us or just get us caught?" I say. Twom ignores me. He runs stop signs and red lights. Horns bleat. Tires gag. Every other moment a collision seems imminent.

And now it is.

Near the busy Saturday-night social epicenter of High

School Highville South, we approach a four-way inter-section. The light is yellow on its way to red, and pass-ing two cars on the right, Twom runs it, yanking the steering wheel hard left. We take the turn in front of the oncoming cars and I'm thrown against the right door as the rear end of the Mercedes breaks out. It suddenly feels as if we're going backward. Metal grinds against metal and the outside mirror explodes as we sideswipe a parked car. Twom counters the slide and I'm thrown back across the seat as we fishtail back across the center line and into the left lane. An oncoming car veers to get out of the way. With nowhere to go, it crashes into the cars that are parked along the curb. There are shrieks and shouts from pedestrians as they leap back out of the way. There are more blaring horns from angry, frightened drivers. Twom whoops with excitement. If he has any kind of fu-ture at all after this night's over, it's in either demolition derby or Nascar.

The inside of the Mercedes is illuminated by street-lights and I can see that Deliza's mouth is half open as if she's panting with arousal. Her hand is in Twom's lap.

Fact.

Five thousand American teenagers die in car crashes annually. There are no statistics as to how many of these crashes are caused by hand jobs.

It seems like a good time to buckle my seat belt.

Once on the interstate, Twom leans on the horn, go-ing around slower cars when he can, blowing up on their rear fender when he can't, riding them, screaming at the top of his lungs as if his yelling will force them out of the way. Deliza, in headache-inducing lioness yowls, urges him on, wild with excitement, ranting about all that's in front of them, the places they'll go, the things they'll do, the babies they'll have.

I want to tell them both that they're delusional, that no matter how fast we go, we'll never escape what's behind us now, not the cops and not the deeds done. But I don't say a word. This is unreality TV and I'm just along for the ride.

As we head toward the S-turn that curves through downtown San Diego, a screaming dragon plummets down out of the night sky, its claws extended to scoop us up. It barely misses.

And then, its wings and tail flashing, its engines roaring and its landing gear down, the plane passes over the highway and continues down into the bright game board strips that are the airfields and Midway District of San Diego.

A plane could take you anywhere. A plane could take you nowhere.

We're doing over a hundred miles an hour as we move into the downtown curve and the Mercedes begins to understeer. We're going too fast for the tires to fully grip the road, and instead of turning, we drift across three lanes before the car regains traction.

My stomach is under the wheels.

The big Mercedes slows just enough for us to make it safely through the bottom of the S, and as we move into the top of the curve, Twom punches it again.

The second patrol car enters onto the highway at Pershing Drive. We go past it as if it's standing still.

As we approach the Coronado Bridge south of downtown, the night takes on a gray quality. It's as if fog or mist has rolled into the harbor from the sea, surrounding the bridge, creating diffuse gray halos around its lights.

Gray is the color of mourning.

The Coronado Bridge is a prestressed concrete and steel box girder bridge that connects San Diego to Coronado Island. It is two miles long. At its highest point it is two hundred feet above the water. The Coronado Bridge is the third deadliest suicide bridge in the United States, obviously used by people who wish to go to heaven confident of their footing.

This is what we do.

Twom looks at me in the rearview mirror. I nod. He looks at Deliza who looks at me and then looks back at Twom.

"Yes," she whispers.

Twom yanks the wheel of the Mercedes and we cross three lanes of the highway just in time to take exit 14A to Interstate 75. The bridge is deserted of cars. Twom takes the center lane and we climb.

Some say death by bridge is an impulsive act. Some, that it's premeditated. After all, there's always time to turn back.

"Do it," I say.

Twom hesitates.

"Do it, baby," says Deliza. She looks excited again.

Twom yanks the wheel. We skid, regain traction. We cross the two outer lanes, accelerating. We don't so much crash through the outside barrier as cartwheel up and over it. I see the airbags bang brutally into Twom and Deliza. The car falls, flipping, and now, through the spiderwebbed windshield, I can see what's below. It doesn't look like water. It doesn't look like anything. We're falling into darkness.

68

Oneirophrenia Rant no. 1

This is the problem. You can be going along. You think you have it under control. Something happens. It's not necessarily your fault. Or maybe it is. Regardless, you try and deal with it. You have no choice. You're now on a trip you didn't ask for. Rapids ahead. Logs and rocks in the water.

Providence.

And how you deal with the logs and rapids is supposed to say a lot about your character. If you're *strong* of character, you'll probably come out okay at the end. Shaken but not stirred. And if you are of weak character, well, that's okay too. In fact, it's totally the point. The trip is supposed to be a *character builder.* It's a test—yes!—and even if you fail, you're going to be all the wiser for it. Better off for the experience. That is, of course, unless you're so weak of character, you fall overboard, hit your head on a rock, and an alligator and a school of rabid fish consume you and you die or, at the very least, end up drinking paint thinner on the streets screaming at imaginary strangers. In which case, all the character building is null and void. Hey, but it sure was a heck of a good learning experience.

Oneirophrenia Rant no. 2

What totally sucks even worse is when you're on this stupid journey of so-called enlightenment and you don't even *know* you are. You're completely in the dark about it. You were going along, doing the best you could, only all the moves you made were absolutely *wrong.* And because you made them, *this* happened and then *that* happened and now, suddenly, here you are, screwed beyond all recognition. And nobody *warned* you. Not your parents or relatives or teachers or advisers or friends, if you had any. How could they? They were in the dark too, dealing with their own character-building journeys. You were supposed to figure it out all by yourself. And guess what? Now that maybe you finally have, now that you sort of get it just a little bit, it's too late to do anything about it. No going back. Inevitable events.

Oneirophrenia Rant no. 3

I swear, if alien ants came to earth, they'd look around at the lack of planning and foresight and the poverty and the greed and selfishness and the ignorance and the intolerance and the overall wasted opportunity that, other than the occasional rare glimmer of light, is the basic human condition, and they'd say, Whoa! Whose great idea was *this?* Unless, of course, they just shook their heads and said, Oh, well, looks like life to me! In which case, the universe really *is* a botched job.

And whose fault is *that?*

69

We're well south of the bridge at National Avenue when the third patrol car comes up the adjacent ramp onto the 5 at speed and falls in beside us. It's like having a ghost at your shoulder. Looking over, the cop studies us. It's hard to tell how old he is. He raises a small microphone and I watch as he calmly talks to someone. I hope he's telling them that we're just kids. Just stupid kids who have made a mistake. Don't blame us. It's not our fault, really. It's this age we're at.

The tragic age.

70

It's almost two in the morning when we come off exit 1A, the last U.S. exit before the San Ysidro border crossing and yet Camino de la Plaza is as bright and crowded and noisy as a carnival. It is bumper to bumper with cruising cars and the sidewalks overflow with people.

We turn left off the exit, nose our way into traffic, and with Twom leaning on the horn the whole way, crawl east on de la Plaza.

Latinas dressed to the nines walk up to low-riding cars driven by guys with shaved, tattooed heads. Peruvian wind instruments compete with Mexican mariachi. There are vendors selling *tacos de cabeza*, which are corn tortillas filled with cow's cheek, and there are old women selling Virgen de Guadalupe medallions and papier-mâché monkeys on surfboards.

It's insane.

We're going nowhere and so we turn right into the first of the large pay parking lots.

The lot is filled with cars and despite the hour—or maybe because of it—seriously drunk Avenida Revolución barhoppers are coming back across the pedestrian border bridge. Most of them are the same grunions from the Pacific Northwest that have been washing up on local beaches—college students on spring break. They stagger down the stairs into the lot, spreading out, trying to find their rides. They move in loud, rowdy, scrambled groups, some so dazed and shitfaced you wonder how any of them will make it home alive.

We pass someone bent over between cars, puking his or her guts out onto the pavement. We pass two blowsy guys supporting a disheveled girl who can barely walk. One of the guys has his hand cupped on the girl's big, saggy boob. They stagger into the driving lane and Twom swerves, barely misses them. The girl falls down. One of the guys yells something drunk and unintelligible.

"Slow down," I say. Twom ignores me and leans on the horn. A group of young men shout at us, swearing, as they leap to get out of the way. One of them pounds on the trunk of the Mercedes as we pass. Twom speeds up.

"Slow down," I say again.

This is the moment when the pickup truck with the huge tires and oversized suspension backs out of its parking place. The chassis of the truck is just high enough to clear the hood of the Mercedes and we plow into the truck bed. As the windshield crushes in, Twom throws an arm in front of Deliza, holding her back. My seat belt and shoulder strap lock, the force of the collision knocking the wind out of me. Twom is not wearing either one and he slams forward into the steering wheel. I hear his single, choked cry and then he falls back, writhing.

"Baby!" Deliza cries out. "*Guapo*, you okay?" She quickly unbuckles her seat belt and turns to him. Twom wordlessly shakes his head. His chin has hit the top of the steering wheel and blood streams from a split. A deep *uhhhhuh-huhhh* is his only sound.

Somehow Twom manages to open the side door. He falls out onto the pavement. He climbs unsteadily to his feet. He is hunched and his arms are across his chest as if he is trying to hold himself together. I get out of the car.

This time I will act.

The first moron who gets out the truck's cab wears a folded-brim straw cowboy hat, pointy lizard boots, and a cut-off sleeveless flannel shirt. The second moron wears a backward baseball cap and a wifebeater undershirt. Both look like they flex their biceps for a living. The driver drops from the cab down onto the hood of the Mercedes and then to the ground, while his buddy comes around the other side.

"Hey shitwad, are you fucking crazy—!"

"What the fuck, you dick suck!"

There are parodies of people like this everywhere. No wonder other people get killed.

This time I will help.

I can't seem to move. Spectators, curious and smelling a fight, are closing in as Twom turns back into the Mercedes and with his right hand reaches under the seat. When he comes back out, he's holding the gun. Twom doesn't say a word. He doesn't have to. Arms raised as if to ward off bullets, the two men are already retreating.

"No problems, hey—it's cool! We're cool!"

They back into a parked automobile. With nowhere else to go, Dick Suck spins and goes around it. The driver, cowboy boots slipping, bolts and runs. Spectators back away. I hear somebody call out. "He's got a gun, dawg, shit, he's got a gun!"

Twom's entire body sags. He lowers his bloody chin toward his chest as if trying to take the pressure off the broken sternum. He totters as if dizzy. Startled, he turns and raises the pistol at Deliza as she comes around the Mercedes. If she so much as flinches, I don't see it.

"It's all right, baby. We walk from here."

It's all Twom can do to nod. She moves to him. Twom gasps in pain as she puts her arm around him. He looks toward me. Blood drips from his chin onto Deliza's cheek.

"You coming, Billy?"

I shake my head.

"Brothers?" he says.

I make sure I say it loud enough so that he'll hear me. "Always," I say.

Twom holds out his free hand, the left one, palm up. I tap it with my own. They turn away. Twom cries out in pain, just once, and then begins to laugh.

"What's funny, baby?" I hear Deliza say.

"I'm not gonna make it," I hear Twom say. As if it's the most hilarious thing in the world.

"Yes you are," says Deliza. "I got you, *guapo*, I got you."

They begin to walk.

I hear the sounds of sirens. As I turn away, squeezing between the two closest cars, I see the police cars turn off Camino de la Plaza and come down toward the lot.

There are buses parked over by the west fence. People are boarding. I have no idea where they're going, but wherever it is, it's better than here. I start toward them.

I've crossed two lanes when I hear the single whoop of a siren. I turn back to see one of the police cars, lights flashing, moving slowly down the lane toward the smashed Mercedes. There are people in the way and a loudspeaker squawks, asking them to move aside.

I climb up on the hood of a car. *I need to know.*

I can see Twom and Deliza walking east toward the stairs that lead to the pedestrian bridge. Twom is leaning on Deliza for support. I see a group of rowdy alpha boys approaching them.

"Yo, babe! Who's the crip?"

I see Twom raise his right arm, the hand that holds the gun. The morons shout and scatter to get out of the way. Twom and Deliza continue on, both of them going faster now. I actually think for a moment that they might make it. Up and across the bridge and they're home. Deliza has people there.

"That way! They went that way! Down there!"

I turn to see the driver of the monster truck, waving at the police car, gesturing down toward the bridge. Back at the gate, sirens whoop again, and I see one police car drive left toward the north perimeter of the lot as the other races toward the south.

The policemen near the Mercedes have gotten out of the car and are moving at a fast trot toward the pedestrian bridge. I jump off the car hood and run in the same direction. There's nothing I can do, nothing I can fix, but I have to try.

All events are influenced by creative acts of the soul.

I push through and into and around groups of people. That they don't know what's happening not even one hundred yards away, that they're so drunk and oblivious, makes me crazy.

"Move!" I scream. "Get out of the way!"

They yell back at me and curse me and push at me as if *I'm* the one in their way.

"Stop! Right there!"

It's the sound of a police bullhorn. Again I scramble up on the hood of a car and move up onto the roof. One cruiser is nearing the pedestrian bridge, the other, coming from the south side, is blocked by cars trying to exit the lot. Twom and Deliza have stopped.

"No farther! We know who you are!"

"No you don't!" I scream. "How can you? None of us do!"

"Hey, get off my car, you sketchy asshole!" I look down at two drunk girls. Fat and skinny. Wobbly and wobblier.

"Put the weapon down and lie down on the ground," says the bullhorn. "I repeat, put the weapon down!"

"I said get off my car, creepo!" Wobbly grabs at my feet and I kick at her and miss. "Ow," squeaks Wobblier as Wobbly nonetheless sinks like a deflating bubble to the ground.

I look back to see Twom hugging Deliza fiercely. I see him push her in the direction of the bridge. She resists and tries to hold on to him. He pushes her again, pushes her so that she falls back and down. She calls his name as he turns back toward the approaching uniforms.

"Put the weapon down, this is your final warning!"

"Make me!" Twom shouts. And then he's running toward them, running fast as only Twom can run, as if the broken bone and the blood on his face don't exist. He has the gun raised and he's firing without aim, the sound of the shots surprisingly soft pops in the night, and in my mind's eye I can see that the flower tattoos that sleeve his forearm, flowers that are the symbols of youth, life, and victory over death, have faded in the bright lights of the parking lot to lifeless gray and black.

The policemen go to their knees as a windshield bursts to the side of them and perhaps it's fear or perhaps it's training and probably it's both but they return fire. Twom is hit mid-stride. In a single instant, he goes from balanced gait to spastic puppet steps, his legs no longer working properly as if he doesn't own them anymore.

Point of fact.

A pilot, caught in a death spiral, never knows he's falling to his death until he hits the ground. Which means he never knows at all.

I hear Deliza wail. I see her get to her feet and run toward Twom's body. Just like in front of High School High, she never stops screaming. Maybe this time she thinks screaming *will* wake the dead. She tries to pull Twom up, pull him to his feet. She might as well try to lift a sack of wet flour. When she sees the cops approaching, she tries to find the gun. They're on her as she grabs it. They pin her down onto the pavement as she tries to shoot them, shoot herself, shoot anyone and anything, screaming all the time. Screaming. Screaming.

I want to go to sleep.

The next moment I'm on the cement. Wobbly and Wobblier have gotten into their car, and as they back out of the parking spot, I've fallen off the roof onto the hood of the car and then off the hood onto the ground. My hands and knees are bleeding but I don't feel it. I don't feel anything.

I get up and, mask firmly in place, begin walking slowly in the direction of the passenger bridge. I have nothing better to do now.

"That guy! He's one of them!"

I walk faster.

"There! That punk right there!"

Several officers look up.

"Him with the face!" someone shouts.

I keep going. Up ahead, the two officers by the parked car start forward to intercept me.

"Sir, you need to stop!"

I pretend I don't hear them. I pretend they're talking to anybody but me.

"Kid! Stop and put your hands on the nearest car!"

I turn and run for the south fence. It's ridiculous. I'm running toward Mexico. But all I can do is run.

It starts now.

Beneath the cacophony of bullhorn, sirens, and voices I hear the sound of someone or something falling. Which is no sound at all. And so I give it one. I give it the sound of drums.

A guy grabs for me and tries to stop me. I tear away from him but it slows me down. I clamber up and over a car. I look back. The policemen chasing me are getting closer.

As the drumsticks beat out a jagged rhythm on the rack toms, someone or something is falling.

I get to the fence. I leap up and begin to climb. The razor wire slashes my fingers and punctures my palms.

The tonal register of the toms is falling.

Someone grabs my legs. I kick at him but he's too strong. He holds on. And then other hands grab me.

I hear escalating rim shots falling on a hollow snare.

My hands and arms are cut to shreds as they pull me screaming and struggling off the fence.

Twom's body is on the ground.

The tenor of the drums deepens as the jagged single rolls move to the first floor tom—

Deliza is sobbing.

—fall to the second—

Ephraim is laughing.

—finish on the third.

As the police surround me, holding me down, which is stupid because there's no longer any reason to, I finally hear what I've been waiting for. It sounds like the deep, muffled thud of a bass drum.

Impact.

71

Supposedly it took God six days to create the earth. He was catatonic on the seventh.

Fact.

Catatonia is a condition marked by a deficit of motor activity. People avoid bathing and grooming, make little or no eye contact with others, can be mute and rigid, and neither initiate nor respond to social behavior.

Sidebar.

Patients in a minimally conscious state can show characteristics very close to that of normal sleep in a healthy subject. They can show changes in "slow wave" activity in the front of the brain, which is considered important for learning and neural plasticity. These patients can also produce NREM, nonrapid eye movement, slow wave sleep, and REM, rapid eye movement sleep.

Translation?

They dream.

And so it is that when I open my eyes Dorie is sitting in a chair across the room. She has the kindest face in the world.

"Hi, Billy."

"Hi, Dorie."

"Love you."

"I love you too."

She stands. She holds out her hand to me. Rising from the bed, I take it. Dorie turns and leads me through the open doorway. She takes me out into the hallway, which is a road. She takes me home. She takes me to the house from the photographs, the one in Tulare, the one where Mom grew flowers, the one we lived in before fate took over. The house where the two of us were born. There is no one there but us. No Mom. No Dad. No Beatrix, Frank, or Lorna. There is no furniture in the house. Instead, the small rooms are filled with drums. Drums of all kinds. Drums of all different sizes. New drums. Old drums. Broken drums.

"Inside of these are all the things that box you in and hold you back," says Dorie. "Shall we open them?"

"No," I say. "This is just a dream. This is my brain spouting useless information."

"Oh, Scarecrow," Dorie says. "If you only *had* a brain."

We open the drums one by one. We pull off the heads and look inside. It takes a long time to open all of them. Every time I think we're finished, Dorie leads me to another drum-filled room. It takes us days. Weeks. Years. But we go to every room and we open every drum and in the end I know what's in every one.

"They're empty," I say.

"Surprise," says Dorie. "Every one. Except this one."

She turns and she points and I see that there is one

last drum sitting in the middle of the floor where it hadn't been before.

"Play it," says Dorie.

I do a roll on it with my fingers. The drum has a deep, good sound. It sounds like a hollow log by a fire.

"Nice," I say.

"Open it," says Dorie.

I do. I take the lid off. I look inside. The drum is filled with tiny shards of shattered glass.

"Pour it out," says Dorie.

I upend the drum and the bits and pieces of glass fall silently to the ground. They lie there, piled for a moment, and then they begin to melt. They form a shimmering, silver circle on the floor, a circle that is a symbol of God, whose center is everywhere and whose circumference is nowhere.

"Now look," says Dorie.

I look down into what is now a mirror and what I see is—

Me.

"Not so scary, is he?" says Dorie.

"No. Just ugly."

"There's no such thing." Dorie smiles. "Are you ready?"

"As I'll ever be."

"Good enough."

Dorie takes me by the hand. Once again, she pulls me out into the world. The last thing I hear as I'm born again is her voice whispering in my ear.

"When you make me an excuse, Billy, you do us both a disservice."

72

Okay, maybe I'm exaggerating when I say I was catatonic, but between sleeping pretty much constantly and, when I *was* awake, not really eating or speaking and ignoring everything and everyone, I might as well have been. But then, when I heard one of the doctors talking to Mom about electroconvulsive treatment, meaning shock therapy, I found myself miraculously cured.

It occurred to me more than once in the weeks and months that followed, I'd been catatonic for a long, long time.

The media made a big deal out of everything. As if there was nothing more important in the world to write or talk about. In less than twenty-four hours we had gone from being the Night Visitors to being the Rich Kid Posse. We went viral, all of us. In fact, we had a fervent fan base, a Facebook page, and there were any number of copycat crimes in different cities across the country.

There were all sorts of op-eds and speeches about the so-called millennial generation, the self-entitled generation, the unemployed generation, the "young adults living at home with their parents" generation and the out-of-luck, no-future, generally screwed generation. There were also some editorials advocating gun control but those were pretty much ignored as usual.

I was put under house arrest, which means I was allowed to go home and shut the door.

Grounded!

The justice system works pretty well when you have bucks. Mom and Dad hired expensive lawyers. The lawyers took the case to a public hearing, which pretty much boils down to the court presenting its evidence against you and you getting the opportunity to make all sorts of excuses. The expensive lawyers hired expensive psychologists. One of them, I kid you not, was Dr. Belafonte, who right off the bat said I'd been in a state of clinical depression since the death of my twin sister and that my parents' separation had fueled it. Seizing on the moment, the lawyers immediately asked if I was in danger of becoming emotionally exhausted by the proceedings because at eight hundred bucks an hour they wanted to keep the court dates going for as long as possible. Dr. Belafonte, who was also getting paid by the hour, said yes I was, and we ended up adjourning for the day.

In the courtroom, Frank and Lorna and Beatrix, Mom and Dad, all sat side by side. Having Mrs. Taylor around twenty-four-seven had made Dad realize he didn't really like her all that much and he'd already been looking for an excuse to come back. My arrest was totally serendipitous in that it gave Mom and Dad something they could mutually blame themselves for, and in order to do it full-time, they were attempting a reconciliation. The only condition was that Dad sell the wine cellar and stop drinking. It was working out pretty well so far.

Serendipity is another word for fate.

In the beginning Frank and Lorna and Beatrix all started off staying at the house because we had the room. Frank and Lorna lasted three days before Beatrix drove them crazy enough to move to a motel, which Dad, of course, paid for. Two days later, Mom actually worked up the courage to ask Beatrix to leave. Beatrix smiled— *really smiled*—hugged Mom, told her how much she respected her for saying that, and moved over to the same motel where Frank and Lorna were staying so she could drive them crazy some more. Mom and Dad were so pleased, they invited Beatrix to join everyone for Christmas.

On the fourth day of hearings, another psychologist took the stand and the lawyers asked him about Ephraim. Ephraim, it turned out, had been on about a million different mood stabilizers, seizure inhibitors, and antidepressants. The psychologist couldn't discuss what Ephraim's issues were but he did say that Ephraim had been seeing him twice a week for over a year. When asked if Ephraim had had suicidal tendencies, the shrink said it was private information. Which of course meant Ephraim did. Everyone felt very sorry for Ephraim's parents, who went out of their way to say they'd done everything they could for him.

Also during the hearings, Mr. Esposito, the principal of High School High, who it turned out had the first name of Ron, got on the stand to tell everyone, in his surprisingly melodious voice, that Ephraim, Deliza, and I were model scholar-citizens who had come under the influence of another student, one with a criminal past and the personality profile of a charismatic sociopath. In other words, it was all Twom's fault. His grandmother stopped coming after the first week.

Gretchen never came at all. Dr. Quinn had suffered a fractured skull and broken ribs in the fall down the stairs, all of which would heal with time. He declined to press charges. Gretchen changed the number to her cell phone. E-mail messages came back as undeliverable. Letters were unanswered. I didn't really expect otherwise. In fact, it was probably for the best. And if it wasn't, still, it was retribution for all the bad things I'd done.

I did get a nice note from Miss Barber. And John Montebello got on the local news one night and was so arrogant and repulsive, a national news columnist suggested I change my plea to temporary insanity coupled with justifiable attempted homicide.

The expensive lawyers and the expensive psychologists finally worked out a deal with the court that said something to the effect that I would plead guilty to a misdemeanor charge of breaking and entering and in return receive no jail time and a year's probation. Everyone went home relieved and happy, confident that because of my history, my future potential, and the family's good standing in the community, justice had been done. Needless to say, the civil suits with different families got settled for an enormous pile of dough.

Mom and Dad moved up the coast to a place not too much different from the one they'd left. It was a nice house. It had four bedrooms, six bathrooms, a guesthouse, a pool, and a four-car garage. It had a nice view. Dad joined a golf club. Mom found new tennis partners. They settled in.

Sometimes it seemed like they hadn't moved on at all.

73

But I did.

I had no choice, really. Just as I had been touched by Twom's right hand, the one tattooed with "chaos," I had also been touched by his left hand, the one marked "change."

That summer and fall I took a lot of college-level classes. I retook my SATs plus the ACT test the following spring. I did well. Useless information proved to be not so useless after all. The spring and summer after that I applied to a number of colleges for January admissions. Fortunately none of the applications had questions about breaking and entering and I pretty much got accepted to every one of them.

I decided to get away from the West Coast and chose a university in New York City.

That's where I am now.

It's almost bearable.

No. Actually it's really pretty good.

It's a nice place. It has a nice campus, all brick and ivy. It has smart teachers. I like listening to them.

The school has a great chapel. It was built in 1904 and is nondenominational. I spend a lot of time there just sitting and thinking. People play folk music in the vestibules.

It sounds crazy but I'm considering a dual major in philosophy and religion. I'm not going to become a minister or teacher or anything. At least I don't think I am. But I'm interested in how faith, or the lack thereof, has historically affected man's conception of himself and his existence.

Why are we so tough on ourselves? Why, if we have faith in God, does *He* have so little faith in us?

When I'm not in the chapel or in classes, I pretty much spend most of my time in the college library. I'll still read just about anything, but these days if you ask me what I'm reading and I think you're serious, I might even talk to you about it. Especially if you're buying the beer.

I avoid the Internet, newspapers, and all television as much as humanly possible.

People talk about a lot here. Sometimes they're even serious about it. Technology will save the world. Soccer will save the world. Social justice will save the world. Idealism will save the world. Cold fusion, music, women's track teams, and alien ants will save the world. The desire to save the world will save the world.

I occasionally get recognized but not too often. For some reason, the port-wine hemangioma on my right cheek has faded. It's hardly noticeable anymore. Or maybe it's just that *I* don't notice it. Usually if someone figures out who I am and what I did, they'll ask a few questions and I'll answer as best and honestly as I can and then we'll all forget about it and move on.

I sleep well. When I sleep my dreams don't bother me. Last night I had a dream about Gretchen.

I'm sitting on a bench. When I look up Gretchen is walking across the campus quadrangle. She's carrying a backpack. She's with friends. She's a student here. When I stand up, she sees me and stops. She turns to her friends and tells them to go on without her. They do. And then she's running toward me and I'm moving toward her and there's joy in her face as she opens her arms to embrace me. But then like a projector chewing film, the dream blurred and I woke up.

I would take that dream and be sad the next day anytime.

I think about Twom a lot. I think of him being so nice to the heavy girl, Ophelia. I think about me turning in essays for him. I think of him raising his hand in class because at last he *knew the answer*. I think of him opening the car door that night for Gretchen and me. *Little Red!* I think about him flying, flying, flying away. It's what he wanted more than anything and maybe that's exactly what he did in the end.

I think about Ephraim sometimes. Babbling about his video games. Talking about Superman. Living in his virtual world. Maybe he's living there now. If he is, the avatar he's created looks just like Twom.

Sometimes I even think about Deliza.

"Got your skateboard, Billy?"

The last time I saw her was in a courtroom. My defense had worked so well that Deliza's father's expensive lawyers and psychologists had used it too. She was crying tears of happiness. She was wearing a nun's habit.

No, not really.

She was beautiful, poised, and perfectly dressed. Her dark hair had new streaks of bright blond. But as she turned for the door, her eyes looked right through me. None of this was happening, and if it was, she couldn't have cared less.

I go running every day in the park. I do a minimum of eight miles. I run easily. My stride is long and steady and my breath turns to steam in the cool air.

Oxygen changes things.

Sometimes I stop and stare at the tops of the buildings that surround the park. They look like kings and queens and bishops and knights on a chessboard. I don't have to tell you who the pawns are.

This is what I wish.

I wish I could tell my fellow Night Visitors that I've learned something. I wish I could tell them that there's no hiding from life. No running from life. That no matter how tragic it appears to be, you can't live in fear of life. That other than by dying, there's no escaping life. No matter how many skies have fallen, once you decide you want to live, well . . . *amor fati.*

Love your fate.

Anything less is just not an option.

Acknowledgments

Serendipity is defined as fortuitous happenstance. I mention this because there are so many people who have seemed to arrive serendipitously—meaning just when I needed them—in my writing life. I'm talking about directors and actors, producers and agents, teachers and fellow writers and, most of all, friends. Hopefully I'll have the opportunity to recognize and thank all of you personally one day. In the meantime, the playwright in me would like to acknowledge the early encouragement and support of Lynne Meadow and Jack O'Brien, the screenwriter in me would like to thank the inimitable Jeremy Zimmer, and the fledgling novelist in me would like to say thank you to the amazing Linda Chester as well as to Sara Goodman and all the wonderful people at St. Martin's Press.